### Close quarters—and a close call.

The dozen or so men between him and the side wall scattered like a covey of quail breaking cover, so there was only one man left standing there, not more than ten feet away.

That man was bearded wearing a laborer's rough clothing and a cloth cap. From somewhere inside his bib overalls he had produced a Webley revolver, squat and ugly and, at .45 caliber, as deadly as sin. He was still aiming it at the spot where Longarm's head had been.

Longarm saw the man's finger begin to tighten on the trigger for a second attempt and his eyes widen when he found the place where his target had moved. The muzzle of the Webley moved on line and the hammer began to rise to the pressure on the trigger. Longarm had less than half a second to . . .

His Colt roared, throwing flame and smoke and filling the place with more noise and the acrid stink of black powder burned in close quarters.

The bullet deflected off the heavy frame of the Webley, throwing the revolver and the hand that held it sharply to the right while the slug, knocked off its intended line of travel, sliced open the cheek of the bearded man but did no serious damage to him.

Longarm cursed. So did the shooter. Undeterred, the gunman then brought his Webley back in line with Longarm's belly.

Longarm rose . . . then fired a second time. This time there was no deflection.

# DON'T MISS THESE
## ALL-ACTION WESTERN SERIES
## FROM THE BERKLEY PUBLISHING GROUP

**THE GUNSMITH by J. R. Roberts**
Clint Adams was a legend among lawmen, outlaws, and ladies. They called him . . . the Gunsmith.

**LONGARM by Tabor Evans**
The popular long-running series about Deputy U.S. Marshal Long—his life, his loves, his fight for justice.

**SLOCUM by Jake Logan**
Today's longest-running action Western. John Slocum rides a deadly trail of hot blood and cold steel.

**BUSHWHACKERS by B. J. Lanagan**
An action-packed series by the creators of Longarm! The rousing adventures of the most brutal gang of cutthroats ever assembled—Quantrill's Raiders.

**DIAMONDBACK by Guy Brewer**
Dex Yancey is Diamondback, a Southern gentleman turned con man when his brother cheats him out of the family fortune. Ladies love him. Gamblers hate him. But nobody pulls one over on Dex . . .

**WILDGUN by Jack Hanson**
The blazing adventures of mountain man Will Barlow—from the creators of Longarm!

**TEXAS TRACKER by Tom Calhoun**
Meet J.T. Law: the most relentless—and dangerous—manhunter in all Texas. Where sheriffs and posses fail, he's the best man to bring in the most vicious outlaws—for a price.

TABOR EVANS

LONGARM

AND THE LUNATIC

JOVE BOOKS, NEW YORK

**THE BERKLEY PUBLISHING GROUP**
**Published by the Penguin Group**
**Penguin Group (USA) Inc.**
**375 Hudson Street, New York, New York 10014, USA**
Penguin Group (Canada), 10 Alcorn Avenue, Toronto, Ontario M4V 3B2, Canada
(a division of Pearson Penguin Canada Inc.)
Penguin Books Ltd., 80 Strand, London WC2R 0RL, England
Penguin Group Ireland, 25 St. Stephen's Green, Dublin 2, Ireland (a division of Penguin Books Ltd.)
Penguin Group (Australia), 250 Camberwell Road, Camberwell, Victoria 3124, Australia
(a division of Pearson Australia Group Pty. Ltd.)
Penguin Books India Pvt. Ltd., 11 Community Centre, Panchsheel Park, New Delhi—110 017, India
Penguin Group (NZ), Cnr. Airborne and Rosedale Roads, Albany, Auckland 1310, New Zealand
(a division of Pearson New Zealand Ltd.)
Penguin Books (South Africa) (Pty.) Ltd., 24 Sturdee Avenue, Rosebank, Johannesburg 2196,
South Africa

Penguin Books Ltd., Registered Offices: 80 Strand, London WC2R 0RL, England

This is a work of fiction. Names, characters, places, and incidents either are the product of the author's imagination or are used fictitiously, and any resemblance to actual persons, living or dead, business establishments, events, or locales is entirely coincidental.

LONGARM AND THE LUNATIC

A Jove Book / published by arrangement with the author

PRINTING HISTORY
Jove edition / May 2005

ISBN: 0-515-13944-0

JOVE®
Jove Books are published by The Berkley Publishing Group,
a division of Penguin Group (USA) Inc.,
375 Hudson Street, New York, New York 10014.
JOVE is a registered trademark of Penguin Group (USA) Inc.
The "J" design is a trademark belonging to Penguin Group (USA) Inc.

PRINTED IN THE UNITED STATES OF AMERICA

10  9  8  7  6  5  4  3  2  1

# Chapter 1

Deputy United States Marshal Custis Long paused outside the barbershop and peered in. The place was full, every seat taken and two men stood waiting to take their turn in the barber's chair.

It was Monday morning and everyone wanted a fresh shave to start the week off with, he supposed. He himself wanted . . . a fresh shave to start the week off with. He was also, however, in need of a trim and a dash of bay rum. There was something about the smell of a little bay rum that seemed to drive the ladies wild.

It honestly never occurred to him that there might have been something about himself that drove the ladies wild.

Custis—Longarm to his friends and to a good many of his enemies as well—stood well over six feet tall and had a lean, muscular build with broad shoulders, narrow hips and powerful limbs. He favored a cherished old tweed coat, brown corduroy trousers, gleaming black cavalry boots and a flat-crowned brown Stetson hat.

His hair was seal brown including the sweeping handlebar mustache that he customarily sported. He had brown eyes that women could melt in. Those same placidly friendly eyes would melt men's nerves if anger turned them to cold steel.

Years of living and working out of doors left him deeply tanned and with wrinkles at the corners of his eyes. His face was more craggy than classically handsome.

He really did think it was the bay rum.

And tonight . . . Longarm smiled a little to himself. Tonight he would like to have a splash of that bay rum because tonight he had a little something special in mind.

"Get in line if you want, mister, but don't just stand there. You're blocking my light," the barber called.

"Sorry," Longarm said. "I'll come back later."

He ambled away down the street, in no hurry now as he had gotten an early start for work thinking he would stop in for that trim beforehand. Now with the haircut delayed he had time to relax and enjoy a truly beautiful spring morning.

Denver can be at its finest in the springtime, Longarm reflected. The mountains to the west of the city could be seen through miles of crystal clear air; they looked close enough to reach in an hour while the truth was that it took more than an hour by rail to get there.

The trees were starting to show emerald green buds where leaves would soon flourish, and there were even a few gaudy flowers beginning to blossom in pots that someone tended indoors through the winter and now set out onto porch rails to show off their blooms.

He turned onto Colfax Avenue and continued toward the federal building where United States Marshal William Vail—Billy to his friends and perhaps even to a few enemies as well—kept his offices.

Longarm paused to buy a newspaper from a boy who

was hawking them on a street corner, thinking he could read it at the office while he waited to see what Billy had for him this week. He pulled a slim, dark cheroot out of an inside pocket in his coat, dipped two fingers into a vest pocket for a match and got the tasty little cigar lighted.

"Hey, mister."

"Yes, sonny?" he asked the paper boy.

"Can I see your pistol?" The kid was pointing to the large, double-action .44-40 Colt that rode in a crossdraw holster just to the left of Longarm's belt buckle. Another pistol, a diminutive derringer, lay out of sight in another vest pocket where a watch fob might normally be found. The derringer was soldered to Longarm's watch chain, a railroad grade Ingersol timepiece at one end and the brass framed pistol at the other.

Longarm exhaled a stream of smoke and shook his head. "No, boy. This is no toy for children to play with. It's a tool. Nothing more than a hammer. You should ought to remember that."

The kid grinned. "Yeah, but you gotta be awful close to somebody to bash his brains out with a hammer. With that pistol there you could blow his brains out from across the street, right?"

Longarm laughed. And rewarded the cheeky little SOB by palming the Colt and letting the boy see but not touch it.

"Wow. How many guys've you killed with this gun, mister?"

"Why, I never kill anybody, boy. I'm a deputy marshal. I apprehend them with it. It's just that sometimes they aren't breathing when I get done making my arrest, that's all." He grinned back at the inquisitive kid and returned the big revolver to its leather.

"You're a marshal? Really? Tell me about . . ."

Longarm shook his head and gave the boy a wave good-bye then continued on down Colfax and turned in at the stone steps of the tall structure set adjacent to the Denver Mint.

He was still just a little bit early. Which, considering his usual disregard for punctuality, was apt to cause some comment inside. That was all right though. This was too fine a morning—and the evening held prospects that were too delightful as well—for much of anything to bother him.

# Chapter 2

Billy Vail was bald and had a round, entirely cherubic face. That outward appearance was deceptive. Vail had spent most of his career in the field, first as a Texas Ranger, later in federal government service. He was hard as nails when it counted.

He was also, Longarm thought, one helluva fine boss. He trusted his deputies and would back them up whether the opposition was a criminal with a gun in hand or a pork barrel politician with greed in his heart.

When Longarm was summoned into Vail's office he found the boss, as usual, behind his desk with a pile of paperwork to get through.

"You wanted to see me?" Longarm asked, helping himself to a seat. He and Billy Vail had worked together too long and too well for them to stand on formality now, at least not when they were alone. When strangers were present Longarm played the role of the humble employee hanging on his master's every word.

"Yes, I do. Two things."

"All right, boss. Name them."

"The first is an assignment. Prisoner transport. A county sheriff in Nevada has arrested Tomlin Jones. Does that name mean anything to you?"

Longarm thought for a moment, then shook his head. "Can't say as I recall ever hearing about him, no."

Billy grinned. "I didn't either, at least not that I remember. Henry caught it immediately."

Longarm was not surprised. Henry was Billy Vail's chief clerk, secretary and general dogsbody. Henry had a meek and gentle demeanor but a memory like an elephant and a bulldog's tenaciousness. Damn little ever got by Henry.

"Jones . . . we don't know if that is his real name or not and frankly we don't care . . . is in custody on state charges of embezzlement. As far as we know there are no outstanding federal charges against him. Our interest lies in what this Jones may be able to testify to in the Staley matter. Jones used to keep the books for Staley. It is said he knows where the bodies are buried, and the attorney general is hoping Jones will agree to testify on behalf of the prosecution in return for our help with those state charges."

"If he really has something to say," Longarm said, "that could be a helluva boost to the prosecution, I'd think."

"So does the attorney general," Billy said.

"What's that quote about great minds thinking alike?" Longarm said with a grin. He reached inside his coat for another cheroot.

Kidding aside, though, he was thinking, it really would be a coup if the government could find a prosecution witness with truly compelling testimony to offer. Everything they had so far, or so Longarm understood, was a hodgepodge of hearsay and circumstance. Direct evidence against

Delbert Staley would very likely put the son of a bitch behind bars where he so properly belonged.

For years Staley had been a low-level bureaucrat with the Department of the Interior. Most recently his duties involved overseeing the federal government's purchases of food commodities and treaty goods destined for distribution to a dozen or more Indian tribes between the Mississippi and the Continental Divide and from the Canadian border south to the Arkansas River. It was a large swath of territory and contained the bulk of the country's treaty Indian population.

As chief purchasing officer for the Department of the Interior, Staley held the reins to several millions of dollars.

That would have been just fine except that at some point the man apparently had started siphoning a fair amount of that money into his own very large pockets via kickbacks and outrageously falsified purchase orders.

The United States attorney general wanted Delbert Staley's head on a pike. Longarm did not blame him. One rotten apple like Staley gave every hard working government employee a bad name.

The idea that they now had a good witness who could help put Staley away was welcome news indeed.

"What I need from you, Deputy, is for you to take this Jones person into protective custody and bring him back here so the prosecution team can sit down with him and hammer out a deal.

"You will not . . . I repeat, *not* . . . give the local sheriff any assurances that Jones will be coming back to him. We don't want you tying the prosecutor's hands. They may have to offer him a full pardon for past crimes in exchange for his testimony. I don't know that they will, understand, but I don't want you taking that tool away from them when you are chatting with this backwoods sheriff."

7

"All right. Point taken. I'll try an' keep my mouf hushed, bawss."

"Excellent. That, in a nutshell, is your assignment. The rest, Longarm, is more of a favor."

Longarm could not help but notice the difference in Billy Vail's form of address to him. A moment ago, Billy was speaking to *Deputy* Long. Now it was his good buddy *Longarm*.

"You might say this is a family matter, Longarm. And you do not have to agree to it if you don't want."

"Boss, I don't even know what it is you're asking. First you tell me. Then I tell you. Okay?"

"Yes. Of course." Billy turned his swivel chair around and stared out the window for a moment. "This is difficult."

"Obviously."

"This thing is . . . my wife. I love her, you know."

"Yes, sir. I do know."

"I do not want to embarrass her."

"Of course not."

"There is in her family a . . . how do I put this . . . a rather unfortunate individual. A cousin, you see. Second, third cousin, something like that. But when they were children, he and my wife were the best of friends. More like brother and sister than cousins. Then they grew up.

"Edgar went to university. He became an engineer. Quite respected in his field, I gather. He and my wife kept in touch by mail. Never a month could go by without them writing. Then . . . I can count on your discretion, can't I, Longarm?"

"Jesus, boss, why'd you go an' ask me something like that?"

"I . . . I am sorry, Longarm. Of course, I can count on you. But the taint of this . . . it just kills my wife to think of

8

it. Her beloved Edgar's mind slipped. Too much pressure in his work. Perhaps some horrible blow in his personal life that he was too ashamed to mention in his letters. We may never know the cause of it. We do, however, know the result. Edgar had a complete mental breakdown. He became a lunatic. Had delusions. I don't know what the doctors call it. I'm sure they have many fancy names to describe his condition. What I would call it is quite simply that Edgar became barking mad."

"That's no reflection on your missus, Billy," Longarm said.

"It shouldn't be, but you know as well as I do that there are those who would suspect everyone in the family is afflicted. Or could be."

"Yes, I suppose so."

"Of course it's so. At any rate, poor Edgar was confined in an institution in Utah where he was working at the time when he . . . slipped."

"Yes, sir?" Longarm could not figure out what sort of favor Billy was trying to get to here but it didn't matter. If it would help Billy and his wife, why, Longarm would do it. There was no question about that. Didn't even bear thinking on.

"Two weeks ago, Edgar ran away from the asylum," Billy went on, still staring out the window while he talked, his fingertips steepled beneath his chin. "Escaped is more like it. I gather he could not be trusted with any sort of freedom lest he hurt himself or, God forbid, someone else."

"Yes, sir?"

"He was recaptured in eastern Nevada. Our information from there is scanty but apparently all they could get out of him was my wife's name and address. They identified him from a flyer that was distributed by the asylum where he had been housed for the past several months. He has to be . . ." Billy sighed and turned the chair around so that he was once again facing Longarm.

"What I am asking of you, Longarm, old friend . . . what my wife and I both are asking . . . is that on your way back with Jones you stop and pick up Edgar as well."

"You want me to take him back, boss?" Longarm was frankly surprised. He would have thought the people at the asylum would have been capable of doing that.

"Not exactly," Billy said. "We don't want you to take him back. We want you to bring him back. Here. Not back to be among strangers in Utah. We have found a private institution in Georgetown that will accept him. My wife can visit him there. Even if . . . even if Edgar no longer knows or recognizes her, she would want to do whatever she can for him. She loves him, Longarm, regardless of his mental state."

"I can understand that, boss. Of course."

"I would go myself but I can't get away right now. Not with everything that is going on here. But we trust you. We know you will treat Edgar as gently as possible. So if you could see your way clear to, um . . ."

"Billy, you needn't even ask. Hell, yes, I'll bring him home. It'll be a privilege t' be able t' do something for you and your missus."

"Thank you, Longarm. Thank you." Billy reached into his desk. "Henry has all the information you will need for transporting Jones. All the vouchers and requisitions and whatnot. And I've prepared an envelope here pertaining to Edgar. We've had a lawyer draw up a power of attorney naming you to act on our behalf in any and all matters. You have letters of introduction, cash for travel and lodging and so forth. A letter addressed to Edgar in case he is lucid

10

enough to read and to understand. If I've forgotten any-thing, wire me. I will give you whatever you need."

"Don't worry, boss. I'll take care of it. It won't be no bother at all."

Billy handed over the fat envelope and shook Longarm's hand. "Thank you, Longarm. Thank you very much."

Billy rarely displayed much in the way of emotion, at least not on the personal side of things, and Longarm was feeling a little embarrassed by the time he got out of there.

# Chapter 3

Longarm stopped at the Chinese laundry to pick up his things. He needed clean shirts and underwear for the trip west to Nevada. Once he had done that, though, he was free as a bird until 10:35 tomorrow morning. And he knew just how he intended to spend that time.

He had a light supper—no sense in feeling stuffed when he was busy in the saddle later—then stopped at the Golden Boar for a glass of rye and a couple hands of stud poker. By nine o'clock he was front row center at the Atrium Amphitheater, which was neither an actual atrium nor an amphitheater—for the final review of the night. The entertainment would continue into the wee hours but not Nelda Craddock's review troupe. Nelda gave two performances each evening and no more. It was in her contract.

In truth, Nelda sometimes gave more than just those two performances. But the third one was quite private. And involved neither singing nor dancing.

She and Longarm had had themselves quite a party Friday evening. Tonight was to be a repeat performance.

Nelda came onto the stage to cheers and yells and thunderous applause. Lordy, but she was one handsome filly. Bright yellow ringlets formed a halo around her heart-shaped face. An utterly magnificent bosom swelled above an hourglass waist and shapely ass and never mind that the large bits were padded and the waist cinched down to nothing inside a corset powerful enough hold back an avalanche. As Custis Long had very good reason to know.

While Nelda sang and pranced about on the stage, he kept seeing her naked. Liked what he saw, too, he did. The girl was pretty, even without her stage makeup.

Being male, he could not help noticing the girls in the chorus. They were mighty toothsome, too. Young and pretty and fresh. Uniform as to diminutive size and small figure. Which was called petite in polite company, he remembered. All five had brown hair done in ringlets to match Nelda's golden curls. All five wore tan dresses that were short enough to show their stockings to mid-calf. He was pretty sure one of them was new since he'd last seen the show Friday evening. She seemed to have replaced a blond girl who had been a little taller than the others, which was why he remembered her even though his eyes that night had been locked on Nelda.

And were again tonight.

The show was a virtual repeat of the Friday performance and his attention wandered just a bit. By the time the last chord was played and the final notes were sung, Longarm was good and ready for a romp in the sack with Miss Nelda Craddock.

He remained in his seat for a spell, both to give the other audience members time enough to file out of the theater and also to give himself time enough for his hard-on to subside. This was one of those evenings—and Nelda was

14

one of those women—when the front of his trousers would enter a room well before he did.

When nearly everyone else was gone he mounted the steps at the side of the stage and made his way behind the curtain.

"No one's allowed backstage, bub. Go out to the alley like everybody else," a little man in a checkered suit ordered.

"Miss Craddock is expecting me," Longarm said.

"Now where have I heard that shit before?" the theater employee said, sarcasm thick in his voice.

"Friend, I'm sure you've heard it all, but I am telling you that Miss Craddock is expecting me."

A short, chubby fellow with graying hair—what little of it he still had—brushed past Longarm and continued toward the dressing rooms without being challenged.

"What about him?" Longarm asked.

"Mr. Beale is a theatrical booking agent, and I'd be out on my ass before the next strike of the clock if I tried to stop him from going where he pleases."

Longarm gave the fat man a dirty look but as he had already gone by he never noticed.

What Longarm noticed was which door he was headed toward. Beale tapped lightly on Nelda's dressing room door and it was opened to him instantly.

Longarm opened his mouth to speak, to call out to Nelda and get her to tell this officious little prick to quit being so bossy and let Longarm past so they could commence the evening's entertainment.

Before a sound left his throat however he saw Nelda at the door. She wrapped herself around the fat man like a blond snake squeezing a bald mouse and proceeded to stuff her tongue halfway down the fellow's throat.

It did not escape Longarm's attention that Nelda's left

15

hand was rubbing the nubbin that the fat man kept inside his britches. Hell, they were still at the door and she was already working on the buttons of the fellow's fly.

The stage manager must have noticed the performance, too, for he said, "What was this you were telling me, mister? Something about Miss Craddock, was it?" There was a smirk on the little man's face.

Longarm felt himself go cold. He had no idea what his expression was but it caused the stage manager to recoil a full two steps backward.

"My mistake," Longarm said stiffly. "Sorry t' trouble you."

He turned and headed for the nearest exit and even though that involved passing through the backstage area, this time the theater man made no attempt to get in his way.

# Chapter 4

"Allow me, miss." Longarm gave a little half-bow and took a step backward as he pulled the stage door open. One of the chorus girls was just on her way out. He couldn't be sure—they all looked enough alike to be almost interchangeable—but he thought this one had been the second from the right.

Instead of stepping outside, the girl cocked her head and squinted up at him. She looked amused.

"Is something funny?" he asked.

"Yeah, you might say so."

Longarm lifted an eyebrow. Did he have ink on his nose or some damn thing?

"Nelda's always trading up. Everybody expects that. But this time, honey, I'd say she made the wrong choice. Jobs aren't all that hard to come by, but you"—she gave a low whistle—"you're the best-looking piece of man-meat I've seen around here. And she turned you down just so she could give Andrew Beale a blowjob? Shit, honey, that's plain stupid."

"I'm not sure if I've just been given a compliment or an insult," Longarm said. "You say Nelda, uh . . ."

"Honey, the girl would fuck a snake if it could get her a two-week booking as a headliner." She laughed. "Come to think of it, that's exactly what she's doing right now."

Longarm shook his head. You live and you learn, he thought to himself.

"I guess your plans for the evening are shot all to hell," the chorus girl said.

"I guess they are."

"Me, I don't have any plans tonight."

"Hungry?" he asked.

The girl grinned. "Starving." She winked and added, "Horny, too."

"Now isn't that just a coincidence?" Longarm offered his arm and the girl slipped her hand through the crook of his elbow.

The two of them walked side by side out of the stage door and down the alley.

There was something to be said in favor of fucking a dancer, Longarm reflected. They have fabulous body tone and conditioning. And stamina to go with them.

On the other hand there are some serious drawbacks to fucking a dancer; they have stamina to go with that fabulous body tone and conditioning.

Longarm wearily threw his legs over the side of the bed and dragged his aching body into a sitting position. He was drenched in sweat and his legs were trembling. He could see the pale light of dawn sifting past the edges of the window blind. They had been going at it the whole damn night, and he felt like he'd been in a train wreck.

Esme looked . . . well, the girl looked as fresh and feisty as a kitten.

He lighted a cheroot and sat there gulping for air and smoke and took a moment to give the girl some serious looking over.

She was fairly small, five three or four at a guess—although the truth was that he hadn't seen her standing upright all that much—with slim, deceptively powerful legs, a tiny waist and tits that were little more than a mouthful. Her belly was as flat as his and a hell of a lot softer and more interesting.

She had a slender neck, full lips and eyes that held flecks of sparkling gold. Her hair, now that she'd loosened it, hung in soft curls almost to her waist.

The really amazing thing about her was that despite the exertions of the evening, she gave the impression of being virginal, almost angelic.

Perhaps, he guessed, that came from her complete lack of shame. She took delight in her own body. And in his. She seemed a completely happy girl. The truth was that Longarm was damned glad he'd met her. Nelda Craddock thought she was trading up last night? Well, that made the both of them who felt that way. Longarm had been with Nelda. This was better.

"What are you looking at?" Esme asked with a smile. When she smiled there was a simple sweetness about her that delighted him.

He shrugged and smiled back at her.

"Lay your cigar down for a second, can you?"

"Sure."

He placed it on the edge of the nightstand where the coal would not cause a burn mark. He felt the bed sag as

19

Esme rolled onto his side of it. Her arm encircled his waist and she nuzzled his side.

"Here, let me wipe off if you're going to do that. I'm all sweaty."

"I like your sweat," she said.

"You like . . ."

She gave him an impish grin and shook her head vigorously up and down. "I do. I really do."

As if to prove the point her lips parted and the tip of her pink and very active tongue crept out between them.

And very slowly, very methodically Esme began licking the sweat from Longarm's body.

"That tickles," he protested.

"Shhh," she whispered. "I'm thirsty."

"But it tickles. It . . . oh!"

The girl shifted her attention from his ribs to his right nipple and all of a sudden it wasn't tickling that he was feeling.

"I wish . . . I wish I wasn't so worn out, girl, but messing there won't get you nothing but disappointment for you already killed my pecker cold and can't raise the dead."

"Shhh," she admonished him again while continuing to circle his nipple with the tip of her tongue. "Have I ever told you that you talk too much?"

"I don't think so, no."

"Custis, you talk too much. Now lay down here for a minute."

"I already told you that . . ."

"Shhh."

Longarm let her tug him down onto the bed, her mouth never leaving his chest.

She shifted position a little and began to lick his face, his ears, his neck.

"You're salty," she murmured. "I like the taste of your sweat."

"I . . ."

"Shhh."

He shut up. And the truth was that this was feeling pretty damn good and never mind unimportant details like exhaustion.

Esme licked her way back down his torso onto his belly. She lifted the dead soldier and licked it, then moved on to his balls and the soft, exquisitely sensitive flat between his balls and his asshole.

Longarm felt that familiar filling of arousal and was forced to conclude that the soldier might not be dead quite yet.

About that time he was nestled moistly inside Esme's mouth and he both heard and felt her chuckle with pleasure as his shaft swelled with renewed lust.

She continued to suck and fondle him until he was fully erect, then took scarcely a moment to rise and straddle him with one knee on either side of his waist and the length of him plunged belly deep inside her body.

Esme gasped as he filled her. Her eyes took on a look of distant delight and a small smile toyed at the corners of her mouth. She began to pump up and down atop him.

Longarm needed do nothing but lie there and enjoy himself while the girl took her own pleasure. And gave it back to him.

Yes, sir, he concluded. There definitely is something to be said in favor of fucking a dancer.

# Chapter 5

"Can't I talk you into staying just a little longer?" the girl said, wrapping herself around him again. "Just a little?"

"No, dammit, I have a train to catch. Besides, you said you have to get to rehearsal and do your exercises." He winked and kissed her. "Although I'd say you've been doing nothing but exercising."

"Just one more time?"

"I'd love to, dear, but I can't. I told you. I have to be on that train."

"All right then, but come do me again some time, will you?"

"I'd love to," Longarm said. It was the truth, too. The girl was a pleasure in more ways than one—and she was one helluva pleasure in that way, too—but the truth was that he was unlikely ever to see her again. Theatrical troupes wandered all over. And so did he. It was highly improbable that their paths would ever cross again.

"Good." Esme pulled a slip of paper out of a pocket on her kimono and stuffed it into Longarm's coat pocket.

"I've written down our itinerary, what I know of it anyway, and if you happen to be in the vicinity . . ."

He smiled and leaned down to give her a long, deep kiss. "I'll do it, too," he said.

Esme sighed and stepped aside. "See you, Custis."

"Of course you will." Longarm let himself out of the room. And hustled like hell to collect his things from his boarding house and get to the train station in time to catch the 10:35.


Longarm was pissed off. Until he realized how foolish that was. Less than twenty years ago this trip would have taken a long, miserable week or more. Modern rail service had that scheduled time down to two and a half days.

How quickly people come to accept the new . . . and then to demand it, he thought, becoming irritated when something goes wrong.

Like now.

There was a problem on the line somewhere ahead. A bridge, he overheard one of the brakemen say, although he did not know what the exact trouble was. Consequently, the Union Pacific stopped the westbound passenger coaches at a nameless crossroad where as a result a small tent city had sprung up to attend to the needs of travelers and act as a temporary terminus for horses and coaches.

It was nine-something in the evening, and the makeshift camp was lighted by dozens of lanterns hanging on poles jammed into the hard-packed earth.

The railroad's passengers had to transfer themselves and their things to a ragtag collection of stagecoaches, then be shuttled around the work on the rails to meet another train on the other side. Meanwhile, he supposed, eastbound passengers would be moved in the reverse direction to con-

24

tinue their journey on the train Longarm and his fellow travelers just took to come this far.

The repair work would add about eighteen hours to the trip and be a colossal nuisance.

But it still would be a damn sight shorter trip than would have been possible before the arrival of the rails, and Longarm figured he should be grateful for that and never mind the inconvenience.

"All right now, folks. No need to crowd. There's room enough for everyone. Just get in line now and load up onto the first coach in line. You'll be on your way again soon as your coach is full. No need to rush. No pushing, please. The train on the other end won't be going anywhere till everybody has arrived, so it don't matter which coach you get on. They're all going to the same place."

Longarm shuffled along with everyone else, their feet raising puffs of dry, powdery dust so that a thin gray haze hung in the still air and settled onto any stationary object. The haze combined with the flickering lantern light to give everything a slightly unreal appearance, as if there might be ghosts and goblins in the shadows just out of view.

"You'll have a rest stop shortly, folks, but now let's everybody get aboard those coaches so we can make room for the folks coming in the other direction. Keep moving now, please, keep moving. Madam, kindly keep your little boy close beside you. We wouldn't want to lose him in the dark now, would we?"

Longarm thought the conductor sounded like he would not at all mind losing the little brat. The kid had been running up and down the aisle in the cars all the way from Rock Springs, Wyoming, until now which was . . . hell, he was not entirely sure just where they were. Somewhere around the line separating Utah and Nevada, he guessed.

"There will be meals compliments of the Union Pacific at your first rest stop," the conductor called. "Move along, please. Keep moving."

The coaches, more than a dozen of them, were a motley bunch. As they came closer he could see two huge Concords, half a dozen mud wagons, converted army ambulances, even one rickety contraption that looked like it might have been a medicine peddler's rig in an earlier life. He kind of hoped that would not be the transportation he drew.

"Move along, folks, move along, please."

Longarm stifled a yawn and trudged slowly along in line with the others. He just hoped the repairs would be completed before he came back in the other direction. Trying to shepherd a prisoner and a lunatic through this mess would be a real handful.

"Move along now, move along."

Longarm's mood was as sour as his stomach when they finally returned to the Union Pacific tracks. The detour turned out to be seventeen hours of dust and discomfort. And the food available along the way was practically inedible. This did not stop Longarm from eating it—he'd had to make do in unpleasant circumstances more than once in the past—but he damn sure did not like it. Didn't like the way the oat porridge lay like a lump of clay in his stomach, either.

"How far are we from where we left the tracks?" he overheard one of the other passengers ask the new conductor.

" 'Bout twelve miles," the harried railroad official said, "but we got no choice. You can only go where the roads and the bridges permit, y'know."

Jesus! Seventeen hours to travel twelve miles. All he

could do was shake his head and hold his tongue, though. He only hoped the repairs were complete by the time he headed back to Denver with his prisoner and the lunatic.

Aboard the train that had just finished dropping off east-bound passengers, Longarm stowed his gear on an overhead rack and headed gratefully to the smoker car where he could get a jolt of stomach-settling rye, a good cigar and a decent meal. In that order.

Another few days and he would be home and this whole thing would be forgotten.

Or so he thought.

# Chapter 6

Longarm left the train at Fannin, Nevada, and entered a mad-house of activity. Men and wagons swarmed like locusts, and four entire cars of freight were off-loaded onto rigs.

"What's all the hustle and bustle about?" he asked at the barbershop where he had stopped to get a shave. "I never heard of Fannin. Now I get here an' see it's busier than downtown Denver."

"Why, mister, Fannin is gonna be bigger than Denver ever thought of being. Mark my words, sir. This may become the next capital of our fair state."

"Why?" Longarm asked. "No disrespect, but I don't see any mines or other sort o' commerce here."

"You have heard of Grady, no doubt," the barber told him while he smoothed lather onto Longarm's rather bristly cheeks.

"Yes, sir. I'm headed there now. Mining town, I'm told."

"Exactly so," the barber agreed. "Grady is the site of a fabulous mine. Virtually inexhaustible ore body down there. But there's neither fuel nor water to power a mill,

29

you see. Everything has to be brought in. And our Fannin is the nearest way to the rails. All the wealth of Grady has to pass through Fannin first, don't you see?"

"I wouldn't think that would be cause for all that I see out there." He gestured with his cheroot toward the beehive activity beyond the barber's doorway.

"Oh, but that's where you're wrong, friend. Because we can ship in all the coal we need, the mill to process Grady's ore is being built here. And because there will be so much of it, we're also building a narrow gauge railroad to link the two. Grady will provide the wealth but Fannin will get the benefit from it."

"I never knew Grady was such a big strike."

"Oh, it's big, all right. Huge. I'm telling you here and now, mister, Fannin will soon replace Virginia City, Carson City, all those others as Nevada's queen city. I don't mean to brag, mind you, but I happen to be a member of the town council, and we're already talking about an electrification project, possibly a telephone exchange as well. And do you know what I learned yesterday? There's an ice cream parlor going in where Hurlbooth's Hardware used to be."

"No!" Longarm exclaimed, trying to sound like he gave a shit. "But what happened to the hardware? You said this ice cream parlor is where the hardware store *used* to be."

"Oh, Hurlbooth's has had to expand, what with all the demand now that the mill site is being prepared and the railroad is about to be built. Bud Hurlbooth is building a new store. Takes up most of one of those new city blocks at the east edge of town. His old store wasn't much bigger than my shop here. Say, do you want a trim today?"

"No, thanks."

"A splash of bay rum then? Only two pennies more."

"Sure, friend. I'd like some bay rum, I reckon."

"Almost done," the barber said, wiping away the residue of lather from under Longarm's ears.

Grady was seven dusty, bumpy, interminable hours away from Fannin. And when he got there he wondered why the hell he'd bothered. The town wasn't but a year or two old and already its buildings had the warped, weather-beaten look of extreme age.

The desert, Longarm thought. Dry as sand. Roasting in bright sun year in and year out. It was a hell of a place to have to live. But if that was where the money was, that was where men would go to get it. Longarm damn sure did not envy the people who lived here.

"Is there a good boarding house nearby?" he asked when he wearily climbed down from the light coach. It was late afternoon when he reached Grady and, after the rigors of travel, he wanted a drink, a bath and a good sleep—preferably in that order—before he picked up Billy's embezzler and got to work.

"There's not a boarding house in town that's worth a shit, friend, but there's a hotel that ain't half bad. Cost you an arm and a leg, though. Two damn dollars each and every night. An' that's without no food thrown in."

Longarm whistled. Hell, he could do better than that in big, busy Denver. But then that, he supposed, was the point. A city the size of Denver had half a hundred good hotels competing with one another for trade. Grady likely had only the one, and they could count on all the business they could handle.

"Point me to it," he asked.

"I'm goin' that way. I'll take you."

"Then I hope you'll join me for a drink by way of a thank-you," Longarm said.

31

The local fellow smiled. "It'd be rude t' turn down the offer, wouldn't it?"

"So it would, friend. So it would."

Uh huh. The drink first. Then a bath and a good sleep. And tomorrow morning early he would find the local law and take this Tomlin Jones fellow off the sheriff's hands.

# Chapter 7

The morning air of the high desert was crisp, damn near cold, when he stepped out of the hotel lobby come the next day, but it felt good. Invigorating. Longarm himself was feeling a helluva lot better after a sound night's sleep. He stretched and yawned and reached for a cheroot to top off a breakfast that may not have been the best but at least lay warm and satisfying in his belly now.

He turned to his right, went to the end of the block and crossed over to the other side, following the directions he'd gotten at the hotel. Civic pride seemed to be running as strong here in Grady as it had back in Fannin.

"Soon as the railroad gets here, Marshal, we're gonna build us a new courthouse," his drinking companion last night had said. "Brick and stone. We already got the plans drawn up and we'll do it, quick as we can get brick shipped in. We don't want those assholes over in Fannin stealing the county seat away from us, you see."

For the time being, though, the courthouse was a squat little flat-roofed building made of native stone. The county sheriff's office was in a pair of rooms that had been added on to the back of the courthouse. A signboard on the street indicated its presence.

Longarm walked through the wide alley that led between the courthouse and a smithy next door where, despite the early hour, a sweaty bald man with the powerful muscles of a blacksmith was busy fitting tiny iron shoes to a string of burros. The little animals undoubtedly worked in the mines, hauling powder and tools in and ore back out again.

"Howdy," the blacksmith called, dropping the hind foot of the burro he was working on and gratefully straightening his back for a moment.

"Good morning," Longarm returned with a smile. "You're at it early today."

"Every day," the smith said. He did not sound like he was complaining about that. Quite the contrary.

Longarm touched the brim of his hat to the man and turned left to the sheriff's office.

The outer office, housing a desk, a pair of chairs, a large wardrobe and a potbelly stove, was empty. A closed door led back to the cell or cells. Longarm could hear voices coming from in there so he helped himself to a seat and waited. Moments later the door swung open and an older man with a snow white mustache and leathery features emerged. He gave Longarm an agreeable smile and said, "Hello, young fellow. What can I do for you?"

Longarm stood and introduced himself.

"Long. Are you the one they call Longarm?"

"Yes, sir, I am."

"Well, it's a pleasure to meet you, son." He stuck his hand out to shake. "I'm Dave Stone."

34

Longarm stopped in mid-shake and his eyes went wide as recognition set in. "You . . ."

"That's right. Here in Grady, doing the same old things."

Dave Stone was practically a legend. Longarm had never met him, but he had damn sure heard of the man. Stone was a lawman in California during the gold rush and tamed a dozen or more of the boomtowns. He had a reputation for being tough with his fists, accurate with a gun and completely honest.

"I thought . . ."

"That I was dead? Nope. Not yet."

"I thought you were retired," Longarm said, although the truth was that he had, indeed, assumed Dave Stone was dead.

"Son, there's no old-age pension in our line of work, and I don't know about you, but I never saved up very much when I should have." He shrugged. "Not that there was all that much to save. And not that I'm complaining now, mind. I've had a good life. Figure I did some good along the way. A man couldn't want for more than that."

"It's an honor to meet you, sheriff."

"You're very generous, Long. I'm the one who should be saying that."

"Not at all. An' by the way, I'm Longarm to my friends. I'd be honored if you'd call me that, too."

"So I shall then, Longarm. Now what are you doing here? Is there anything I can help you with?"

"I've come about a prisoner of yours."

"That would be Jones, right?"

"Yes, sir. The U.S. attorney back in Denver wants him as a witness."

"In the Staley prosecution," Stone said.

"That's right. But how did you . . . ?"

"I'm the one let your people know that I have Jones, remember? Know why I notified them?"

"It never occurred to me t' ask," Longarm admitted.

"Jones asked me to, that's why."

Longarm's eyebrows went up.

"Tom won't tell me what he's so frightened of hereabouts, but he wants to be taken back East so he can testify against Staley."

"I'd think Staley would have a lot of powerful friends. Rich ones, too. One of them might well be willing to spend a little on a shooter to keep your man Jones from testifying."

"I mentioned that to Tom, but he insists. I'd say he's even more scared of something here than he is of that possibility."

"So you won't oppose my taking him off your hands?"

"Not at all, Longarm. You're welcome to him. The charges we have him on are minor. We're willing to wait to try him."

"Embezzlement is what I was told."

Stone nodded. "He stole a hundred fifty dollars from the Stella Mae mine. Stole it to cover a gambling debt, then was stricken with conscience and turned himself in voluntarily. The whole thing smells to high heaven as far as I'm concerned, but that's what happened, never mind that it makes no sense."

"Must make sense to Jones or he wouldn't have done it," Longarm observed.

"Obviously. Maybe you'll find out about it. If you ever do, I'd appreciate a note to fill me in, because I certainly can't figure it out."

"If I do get it out of him, I'll be glad to do exactly that, Sheriff," Longarm promised.

"Do you want your prisoner now, Marshal, or would you have time for a cup of coffee?"

Longarm grinned. "The stage won't be heading back to Fannin until ten, they said. That should give me plenty of time to drink some coffee and jaw with you. If you don't mind the intrusion, that is."

"No intrusion, son. It'll be my pleasure." Stone rummaged in the wardrobe, which revealed a small arsenal of rifles and shotguns as well as cups, canned milk and a poke of sugar, while Longarm brought out a pair of his best cheroots to share with the man.

# Chapter 8

Tomlin Jones was not the bookish little fellow Longarm thought a bookkeeper should be. He was in his fifties and his hair was graying, but even so he was a big, strapping, handsome fellow who stood eye-to-eye with Longarm and looked like he was capable of dropping an ox with one punch.

"You aren't . . ."

"Yeah, I know," Jones said with a grin when Longarm looked him up and down. "Everybody thinks that. I was on a champion rowing crew in college. Used to go in for a number of sports. I still run to keep in shape."

"It shows. I'm Long, by the way. I'm a U.S. deputy marshal and I'll be taking you back to Denver to testify."

"Pleased to meet you, Deputy Long." The man sounded like he actually meant that. Stone had said he was easy to get along with. Now Longarm could see why.

Longarm took a cheroot out of his coat and extended it through the bars of Dave Stone's jail cell. "Smoke?"

"No, thank you. It's bad for the health, I've read. Cuts

down on the wind. I wouldn't want anything to interfere with my running."

"No, of course not. A little hard t' run inside a jail cell though, isn't it?"

"I don't plan to be behind bars forever," Jones said, then flashed that friendly grin again. "Indefinitely perhaps, but not forever."

"I see what you mean. Let me give you a piece of advice then. The only times I'm willing to run are when I absolutely have to, and I'm not all that good at it. Don't like it, either. It pisses me off and makes my head swim and my chest hurt."

"It's those cigars, if you don't mind me saying so."

"Whatever it's from, I don't like to run. An' knowin' what a runner you are I won't even try an' catch you on foot if you try to run on me. I'll just shoot your legs out from under you an' be done with it."

"I would not much like that, Deputy."

"Then don't run."

"I have no intention of it."

"Which reminds me o' something, Mr. Jones. Sheriff Stone tells me you turned yourself in for embezzlement."

"Yes, sir."

"That makes me real curious, Mr. Jones. Something else does, too. He said you're the one who tipped him that you used to be Delbert Staley's bookkeeper an' know where the bodies are buried. Stone says he wouldn't have known to contact the U.S. attorney about you if you hadn't suggested it."

"Is that right? I guess I assumed he would have prior knowledge about such things," Jones said.

"That wasn't a very good lie, Mr. Jones, but you tell it

with a perfectly straight face. Remind me not t' play poker with you while we're traveling. I think I'd end up losing everything but my boots. . . . an' them only because they wouldn't fit you. You don't want t' tell me why you peached on yourself those times?"

Jones only shrugged. And grinned again. "We can talk about it later perhaps."

"Yeah. Perhaps." Longarm bit the twist off his cheroot and spat it onto the jail floor, then fetched a match out of his vest pocket and lighted the slender little cigar. Jones might well be right about cigars cutting a man's wind. But damn they tasted awful good.

"Feel up to some traveling today, Mr. Jones?"

"Oh, I am quite ready, Deputy."

"Got any luggage?"

"A small Gladstone. Sheriff Stone is holding it for me."

"I'll have t' look through it t' make sure you aren't hiding any guns or knives or anything in there."

"I have no objection to that, Deputy."

"I'll go do that now an' be back in a little while to walk you over t' the stage."

"Very well, Deputy." Jones grinned. "I have no other plans at the moment, so you can expect me to be here when you return."

Longarm closed the door behind him when he went back into Stone's office. "Likeable cuss, ain't he?"

"Very."

"D' you think he's on the level, Dave? I mean, he sure as hell isn't acting like any ordinary prisoner. He's up t' something. Has t' be."

"He has his own reasons for all this, Longarm. He has to. But damn if I can figure out what they are. If you find out,

41

I'd like you to tell me because I'm as curious as you are."

"Got those papers ready for me t' sign, Dave? Oh, and I'll want to go through his bag t' see if there's any contraband in there."

"The release form is here. I've already filled it out except for your signature. And I will want a copy of the federal warrant. While you sign your life away, I'll get the bag. Be back in a minute."

Longarm checked his watch. There was plenty of time to get everything done and make the next stage back to Fannin and the train depot.

# Chapter 9

Jones was visibly relieved when the stage pulled out of
Grady. He sighed and sat back on the thinly upholstered
bench with a contented smile. The only other passenger besides Jones and Longarm was a young fellow with a sample
case on his lap who looked like he ought to be in high
school instead of out on the road selling.

The boy's eyes became wide and then quickly shifted
away when he saw Jones's handcuffs and Longarm's revolver. He looked nervous enough that Longarm guessed
he was likely a runaway with some sort of mischief behind
him. Whatever it was, he'd done, it must have been serious
enough to make some town marshal somewhere interested
in him. Or at least he thought the law back home would
want him. Maybe so, but unless there was a federal warrant
out for his arrest, Longarm was not going to take any interest in him beyond wishing him well.

"Could I ask you a favor, Deputy?"

"The name's Longarm. And yes, you can ask a favor.

Won't know until I hear what it is if I'll give it, but you can always ask."

"I've been cooped up in that jail cell for more than a week. I'd like to get down and run along beside the coach for a few miles." Jones smiled. "You can always shoot me if I get too far away."

Longarm pondered the request for a moment but could see no harm in it. "All right. I'll get the jehu to stop the rig so you can get out."

"Oh, there will be no need for that. Just unfasten these, if you please, so I can swing my arms, and I'll drop out the door while we are moving."

Longarm cast a skeptical eye at the speed with which the roadside rocks and scrub were rushing past, then said, "All right, but don't be thinking that I won't shoot. I won't aim to kill you, but I'd cut your legs out from under you." He reached for a cheroot. "Unless this here coach bounces an' spoils my aim, that is. If that happens I won't be held responsible for where I hit you."

"Fair enough," Jones said.

The young salesman turned so pale Longarm thought he might faint dead away. No sir, whatever the kid did back home it couldn't have been anything a grownup person would think was interesting.

Jones held his wrists out while Longarm fished among the matches in his vest pocket to find his handcuff key and open the bracelets. Longarm folded the handcuffs and dropped them into his pocket. "Stay right beside the coach, mind. I won't bother with no warnings."

"All right. Thanks." Jones grinned and opened the door. He crouched low and felt with his foot for the step while Longarm slid over beside the door where he could keep watch. The salesman shrank away as far as he could get on the other side of the vehicle.

Jones gathered himself, judging the speed of the coach, then dropped to the ground and hit already running.

"I'll be damned," Longarm said as much to himself as to the boy. "I expected I'd have t' shoot him right off, but he's on his feet an' even keeping up with us."

The boy swallowed hard and squeezed his eyes tight shut. Longarm wanted to tell the kid to go home to his mama but didn't.

Jones really was holding his place at the side of the coach, just outside the cone of dust that billowed up behind.

"I'm ashamed of myself," Jones said at the lunch stop.

"For robbing your employer?" Longarm asked.

"Oh, good Lord, no. For not being able to run more than three miles or so out there. I should be able to go five or six miles at that pace. I'm getting out of shape from sitting in that cell."

"You didn't look it t' me. Say, I'd think you'd be hungry after all that exercise though. How come you aren't having anything to eat? I grant you it isn't anything special, but it ain't bad either."

Down at the other end of the long table the kid salesman was wolfing down a bowl of stew and seemed bent on emptying the plate of squaw bread all by himself.

"I'm embarrassed to tell you this, but I have no money to pay for a meal. Sheriff Stone confiscated my available cash and placed it in escrow pending trial. The court could well order me to pay restitution, you see."

Longarm snorted, then raised his voice. "You there. Bring this man his meal, will you?"

"He said . . ."

"I know what he said an' now he's changed his mind."

"Please, Deputy. I don't want to burden you and . . ."

"Oh, hush. I ain't paying. The U.S. government is. You're in protective custody as a witness. That makes us responsible for your health an' well-being while we have you, same as the county was responsible for feedin' you back in that jail cell. So eat up. I won't be buying you no liquor but other than that, mister, you're gonna eat and drink as good as I do."

Jones smiled. "Well, in that case, uh, could I have two bowls?"

Longarm laughed. "Station keeper," he called out. "Make that two bowls o' your stew, please."

# Chapter 10

"Damn! Tomorrow?"

"That's right, sir. You missed the last eastbound by twenty minutes. Sorry," the railroad ticket agent said. He sounded bored, not sorry.

"When's the next one then?" Longarm asked.

"In the morning. The first passenger cars are scheduled at seventeen minutes past seven. There will be another eastbound at nine twenty-four if that is too early for you or an afternoon train at one thirty-two. Would you like tickets?"

Longarm showed his badge. "I'll be traveling on this, thanks. Quarter past seven you said?"

"Seventeen past."

"Yeah. Whatever. We'll be . . ."

Something dropped on the platform outside. Whatever it was landed with a loud bang, and Longarm's prisoner jumped behind the ticket agent's counter.

Jones was pale and shaking even before the front sight of Longarm's Colt nestled in the hollow beneath his chin.

"I—I—I'm not . . . not trying to run. Oh, God! I—don't

shoot me. Please don't shoot. I'm not trying . . . I thought someone out there shot at me. I thought . . ." He shuddered.

"Why'd you think someone fired a gun, Jones? An' if anyone did shoot, why would you think it was at you?"

Jones shook his head nervously and came to his feet, peering cautiously at the open doorway and then at each of the two windows that faced out onto the railroad depot platform.

There were people out there milling about and talking, some working at moving freight and packages around. No one was paying the least bit of attention to Longarm and Tomlin Jones except for the young salesman who had walked a few paces behind them on the way from the stagecoach offices to the depot. He was staring at them with obvious mistrust.

"Pick up your bag, Jones. We're gonna have to get a room at a hotel for the night."

As they were on their way out Longarm overheard the salesman say, "One ticket eastbound, please. On one of the later trains, not the seven-seventeen one."

The ticket agent smiled. "Not an early riser are you?"

"Yes, sir, something like that."

Longarm guessed the kid didn't want to risk being in the same car as the two madmen he'd ridden with from Grady, the one who got out of the coach and ran for miles and the other who was eager to shoot someone.

Longarm smiled a little. Wherever the boy was going he would have some tales of dangerous adventure to tell when he got there.

"Where are we going now?" Jones asked.

"The jail. I'll put you safe in a cell overnight and go find me a place to sleep," Longarm told him.

48

Except, he discovered, Fannin was in the process of building a huge new jail. They were putting it in a huge new city hall building that looked suspiciously like what a county courthouse should be. Apparently, the folks in Grady had well-founded fears about Fannin stealing the county seat from them.

That of itself was fine, Longarm thought. He really did not give a shit which of the miserable high desert towns won. Except some stupid SOB sold the old city hall building to a high rolling investor, and, at least for the time being, Fannin had no jail of its own.

"But where . . . ?"

"It's no problem," Longarm assured him. "We'll just go get a room for the two of us."

Uh . . . no.

Because of all the activity and growth, Fannin's two hotels were already bursting at the seams, with not a room to be had in either of them. Nor was there space in any of the three boarding houses they checked.

"What are we going to do?" Jones asked. He sounded quite apprehensive at the thought of spending a night without a proper bed.

"No problem. We'll sleep in the livery barn." Longarm lighted a cheroot and found the Fannin livery, which seemed to be doing a booming business.

"No!"

"Pardon me? We haven't even asked a question yet," Longarm told the man at the livery.

"Don't have to. Walkin' around carryin' yer damn suitcases, I don't need no question asked. You came lookin' for a hay pile t' sleep in, din'cha?" The man turned his head and spat a stream of dark tobacco juice.

"I guess we did at that."

"An' the answer is no. Which I already tol' youse."

"But . . ."

"No buts or ifs or none of that shit, sonny. The answer's no. Gonna stay that way. Know why? I see you smokin' that son-of-a-bitch *see-gar*. Last bastard I let sleep in my hay swore on his mama's grave he wouldn't go to smokin' in my loft. Swore it up an' down. Good thing I happened t' be comin' home about the time he fell asleep smokin'. I lost more 'n twenny-five dollars worth o' good grass hay that night an' coulda lost th' whole damn shebang. Since then ain't no smoker been allowed an' never mind what the son of a bitch promises. Th' answer is no. Trust me. Ain't gonna change."

Longarm sighed and thought about the likelihood of a bribe changing the fellow's mind. "All right, sir. Thank you for your time."

"Lordy, Deputy," Jones said as they were walking away. "Couldn't you have done something to force him to house us? I'm a prisoner, you know. You have to put me up, don't you?"

"Now just what was I gonna do? Arrest the fellow for trying to keep his barn from burning down? Mr. Jones, I can be real creative when it comes to thinking up things to charge people with, but that one woulda been too much even for me. Don't worry about it. We got one more chance. We'll check the saloons. Might be someone will have a crib they aren't using."

"Crib?"

"You know. A place where the whores work."

"I . . . wouldn't know about anything like that," Jones said. Said it quite primly, too, he did. So much so that Longarm actually believed him. Tomlin Jones really did not know anything about whores and their habitats.

Trying the saloons was no doubt a fine idea. But a fruit-less one.

"Mister, I already got every bed I own rented out, some of them twice, and about all the floor space, too. Sorry. Try down the street."

It was the story they got everywhere they went. Even the display of his badge and the promise of a government voucher did no good.

Finally Longarm gave up. It was already well past dark, and he was both tired and hungry. And beginning to be more than a little pissed off. "We'll get ourselves some supper an' go sleep on a bench over at the train depot."

"Outdoors? Where just anybody can see us?"

"Yes, Mr. Jones. Outdoors. Where just anybody can see us."

Jones was not a happy man. Which did not keep him from wolfing down enough food to stuff two grown griz-zlies and a cub as well. If nothing else, Longarm thought, the man could eat. If he kept that up after he stopped his running, he would soon be the size of a grizzly.

Longarm paid for their meal, and the two of them picked up their bags.

The train depot was only a block and a half away from the nameless café where they'd had supper. There were three saloons between the café and the depot. Longarm turned in at the first of them.

"What . . . ?"

"I want a drink before we sleep. Settles my stomach. I suppose you aren't a drinking man?"

"I'll enjoy a brandy once in a while, but I never imbibe to excess."

"No, I thought not," Longarm said. "In here, then. Bar-keep, we'll have one brandy an' one rye whiskey. Maryland

51

rye if you got any. Pennsylvania would do next best. And if . . ."

He never got the rest of the words out.

Behind him there was a loud shout of, "Long! Damn you," and the reverberating explosion of a gunshot, incredibly loud in such close quarters.

A stack of glasses on a shelf behind the bar shattered, shards of glass flying in all directions.

Longarm neither saw nor heard any of that though.

He had already dropped into a crouch and was spinning to face the shooter, his Colt in his hand and rising.

# Chapter 11

At first, Longarm could not see who had shot at him. The dozen or so men between him and the side wall scattered like a covey of quail breaking cover, throwing themselves in all directions. Well, all directions except up, and, in one fellow's case, maybe that, too. So there was only one man left standing there, not more than ten feet away and likely not that far.

That man was bearded, wearing a laborer's rough clothing and a cloth cap. From somewhere inside his bib overalls he had produced a Webley revolver, squat and ugly and, at .45 caliber, deadly as sin. He was still aiming it at the spot where Longarm's head had just been.

Longarm saw the man's finger begin to tighten on the trigger for a second attempt and his eyes widen when he found the place where his target had moved. The muzzle of the Webley moved on line and the hammer began to rise to the pressure on the trigger. Longarm had less than half a second to . . .

His Colt roared, throwing flame and smoke and filling

the place with more noise and the acrid stink of black powder burned in close quarters.

The bullet deflected off the heavy frame of the Webley, throwing the revolver and the hand that held it sharply to the right while the slug, knocked off its intended line of travel, sliced open the cheek of the bearded man but did no serious damage to him.

Longarm cursed. So did the shooter. Undeterred, the gunman then brought his Webley back in line with Longarm's belly.

Longarm rose and took a step to his left, it being far more difficult for the shooter to track a target in that direction, then fired a second time.

This time there was no deflection. Longarm's bullet entered the base of the shooter's throat and passed completely through, splattering the side wall of the saloon with blood and bits of meat and bone.

The man dropped to his knees. His hand closed reflexively on the grip of the Webley and discharged a round into the floor where the flame of the burning powder touched off a small fire. The fire was quickly extinguished when the body of the shooter fell on top of it.

Longarm rose to his full height, the muzzle of his Colt searching back and forth like a viper seeking out prey, but there was no other threat to be found.

In fact, there were practically no other people around. The crowd that had been there moments before had nearly disappeared.

"Son of a *bitch*!" Longarm growled. He took measure of each man who remained in the place and, when he was satisfied none of them wanted to draw cards in this game, reloaded his Colt.

Only then did he notice that Jones was down on the

floor with his arms covering his head. Longarm nudged his prisoner with the toe of his boot. "You can get up now. The fun's over."

Jones did not respond, so Longarm tried again, tugging on his sleeve until Jones moved his arm enough to peep out with one eye.

"Get up. It's all right now."

Jones looked reluctant but he sat up. He seemed positively stricken when Longarm left his side to take a closer look at the dead man.

The fellow had fallen face down. Longarm rolled him over and looked at him closely, then shook his head. He had no earthly idea who this man was—or had been—or why he took that shot. Revenge for something Longarm did in the past? A wanted felon who thought if Longarm was here in this room then surely he must be there chasing this poor dumb SOB? It could have been anything.

Longarm briefly checked the dead man's pockets but there was nothing there that would identify him. He had a little money, a bandana, a pocket knife, a plug of chewing tobacco and a room key.

Longarm looked at Jones, who had gotten to his feet and was brushing himself off. He grinned. "If I knew what room that key fit, we'd go sleep in it tonight."

Jones did not react.

Longarm raised his voice. "Anybody know this fella? Anybody got a name for him?"

The place was starting to fill up again as spectators crowded in to get a look at the blood and the body on the floor and the flecks of gore that were stuck to the wall, but if anyone knew who the recently deceased was they were mum about it.

"Hey, you," the bartender bawled.

"Me?" Longarm asked.

"That's right. You. What are you going to do about that mess?"

"Not much," Longarm said. "I'll ask around tomorrow to see if anybody can identify him, I suppose."

"I mean what are you going to do about that body?"

"Oh, I reckon I don't need it for anything. You can have it."

"I meant . . ."

"Look, mister, I know what you meant, but I don't know what services you got in this town or how to find a deputy or an undertaker. But I bet you do. Call for whoever is needed when you figure the poor bastard has laid there long enough. In the meantime, you'll be sellin' beer fast as you can pump it what with all the ones wantin' to come gawk at the scene of all the excitement."

Longarm felt a tug on his sleeve. It was Jones. "Did I hear you say you will be staying over tomorrow because of this?"

"That's right. I'm to take you back, Mr. Jones, but there's no great rush about it. The U.S. attorney an' the grand jury is gonna be there a spell. A day or two either way ain't gonna make no difference."

Jones went even more pale than he already was, which Longarm would have thought impossible if he hadn't seen it for himself. "I . . . we can't."

"Can't what?"

"Can't stay here any longer. Really."

"Oh, I don't see why not, Mr. Jones," Longarm said, picking up the glass of rye he'd been forced to abandon a few minutes earlier. "Damn, that does taste good." He wiped his lips with the back of his hand and dipped his beak for a second opinion. But he'd been right the first time. It did, indeed, taste almighty good.

"But you don't understand. I have to get away from here. I . . . thank you for protecting me just now. But . . . please . . . we have to get away from here. As quickly as possible. They . . . they're trying to kill me, don't you see? They failed this time, but they will try again. Please. If you want me to live to testify, get me away from here at once. Tonight, if possible. The very first thing in the morning, if necessary. But get me away from here, deputy. My life depends on it."

# Chapter 12

"All right now, dammit. Tell me," Longarm said when he got Jones alone and out of sight. With every business in town humming with activity and every room rented out twice over, the best Longarm could do toward achieving privacy was to find an uninhabited alley. And even those were hard to come by here, he'd discovered.

"Tell you what?"

"Tell me why anybody here would give a shit about a penny-ante embezzler?"

"I am *not* a . . ."

"Fine. You're a fucking genius embezzler who just happened to get caught with his hand stuffed in the till after only . . . what was it? A hundred fifty bucks someone said you took?"

"That was only an excuse," Jones said: "I turned myself in, remember? And if it matters, I never stole a red cent from my employers. That was a lie I concocted myself."

"Now why would an innocent man turn himself in for a crime he never done, Mr. Jones?"

"Protection, Deputy. I need protection from . . ." Jones stopped and peered carefully around then lowered his voice. "I need protection from the owners of the Stella Mae."

"Now you're really confusing me. Stella Mae?"

"That is the mine I worked for. Well, one of them. There is a conglomerate of three mines, actually, but the Stella Mae is the largest mine in the district, the original strike and far and away the largest employer in this entire part of the state."

"All right, but what does this have t' do with you turning yourself in for embezzlement when you're now sayin' you are an innocent man?"

"I see . . . no, that is no longer correct. I saw . . . used to see . . . all of the company records. Including production reports and all income and expenditure statements. Do you understand? I had access to everything."

"Go on." Longarm reached into his pocket for a cheroot, then remembered they were trying to hide in the alley here. Striking a match would only call attention to them and probably upset Jones as well. He settled for gnawing on the slim roll of tobacco instead, although that was far from providing the pleasure that a good smoke could give. Sort of like fingering a woman's pussy when what you really wanted to do was poke it.

"I discovered that the Stella Mae is fast fading into oblivion, Deputy. The ore bodies are yielding less and less. Already the mine is yielding less income than the production costs to get the metal out of the ground. Normally one would expect the mine to close at that point, but the managers apparently want to convince the investors that everything is as it used to be. No production reports are being released now, and the investor dividends are still at their previous levels, too. In short, the investors are being defrauded. Kept on a string, if you will."

"Why would somebody want t' do that, Mr. Jones?"

"Understand, please, that I did not handle the personal accounts of the managers, Deputy, but I have reason to believe that what little income is now being generated is expended on one of two things. The so-called dividends and the pockets of the managers themselves. Remember, I saw the outflow of cash as well as the income. Suppliers and contractors are no longer being paid, sir. Bills are piling up, but only excuses are being sent out. The expenditures that are being made are being made to dummy companies that . . . and this part is speculation, I admit . . . that I believe to be owned by the Stella Mae managers who were hired to see to the well-being of the mine and of the absentee investors. Do you understand what I am saying, Deputy?"

"Sure. But why would anybody want t' kill you about this? You ain't the one as made that ore body dry up."

"But I am the only one outside of the management who *knows* about it, sir. And . . . and the other two mines are beginning to falter in their production values as well. What I am saying, sir, is that the entire Grady district is only a flash in the pan. Within six months the town of Grady will no longer have any reason to exist. It will wither and fade away just as so many other boomtowns did before it."

Jones waved his hand to encompass everything around them in the gesture. "All this construction in Fannin? It is doomed just as completely as is the mining district. Oh, Fannin may hang on as a watering station, on the Union Pacific, but it will attain none of the expected commercial success that it is building to meet. All of this"—he shook his head—"it is wasted, sir. Wasted and doomed."

"Shit," Longarm said.

Jones gave Longarm a wan, tired smile. "Exactly, sir. Exactly."

"But this still don't tell me . . ."

"They want to kill me for two reasons, Deputy. Exposure of their game at this point would keep them from filling their pockets with what little remains to be had from the mines. And second, but not necessarily the lesser of those reasons, is that premature disclosure . . . before they can hie themselves beyond the reach of their fellow citizens in Grady and in Fannin . . . would allow the mobs to find them."

"Mobs?"

"Believe me, Deputy, when the news sinks in, when people here know that they have been duped by those scoundrels, they will want someone to punish for the shattering of all their hopes and plans and dreams. There will be mobs. The managers want time to escape before that happens, to escape as wealthy men in their own right and not simply as employees hired to safeguard someone else's wealth.

"I know the truth, you see. I am capable of foiling their evil design. Naturally they want me out of the way. That is why I fabricated that story about an embezzlement that I did not commit. It is why I turned myself in to Sheriff Stone and confessed to something I did not do. I knew he would protect me. I also knew, though, that the farther I can get from Grady, the better. And that is why I suggested that the sheriff contact the authorities in Denver."

Jones smiled, this time the expression a full and a bright one. "You, sir, are my protector, albeit unwittingly. And that is the reason for the attempt on my life this evening. I fear there may be more. They will not want me free to disclose their plan, and the only way to be sure of silencing me is to put me in a grave. I apologize for putting you in the middle of this, sir, but I pray you will not abandon me to the assassins they will send against me."

Longarm absently flicked a match aflame and lighted his cheroot. After a moment's reflection he said, "Nobody's gonna kill you, Jones. Not while I'm alive. Now come on. We're gonna get some sleep."

"On the open platform?" Jones sounded worried again.

"No, under the circumstances, I reckon what we will do is wake up the railroad telegrapher an' get him to open the station office for us. We can bed down there on one o' the benches. That will do till morning an' time for that early train east."

"Thank you, Deputy. I am in your debt."

"Mr. Jones, gettin' you back t' testify is my job. You'll do that best if you're still breathin' when we get there. Now pick up that bag o' yours an' lets go find us a place to get a little undisturbed shut-eye, shall we?" Longarm drew in a long, satisfying drag on his cheroot, then looked both ways before stepping out of the alley mouth.

You never knew when or where some other son of a bitch would want to collect whatever bounty had been placed on Tomlin Jones's head.

# Chapter 13

"What do you mean we have to leave the train here?" Jones complained. "Don't you know . . ."

Longarm silenced him with a dark, glowering look. Jones had been whining most of the day. He didn't like the food. A hot cinder that flew in through the window burned the back of his hand. He was getting motion sickness. He was . . . he was making Custis Long pissed off is what he was doing.

"I have business in Salt Springs," Longarm said. "That's why we have to leave the train here."

"How long will . . ."

"As long as it takes, that's how long," Longarm snapped. The truth was that he had no idea how long it would take to get to this Salt Springs place and pick up Mrs. Vail's cousin Edgar Bowman. Hell, he didn't even know for sure where Salt Springs was. When he left Denver he'd been under the impression that it was somewhere along the railroad right-of-way and he could just take a brief layover between trains to get hold of Edgar and get back onto an eastbound.

Now he learned from the conductor that the town was somewhere north of the railway up in the Thousand Springs area. Wherever that was. Lordy, the things a railroad conductor was required to know. It was not a job Longarm envied.

He pulled out a cheroot, ignoring Jones's disapproving frown, and lighted up. After just two days in the man's company, Tomlin Jones was wearing a mite thin.

Of course, Longarm had been required to transport much more annoying prisoners than Jones was. Prisoners, for instance, who were intent on killing him if they got the least chance. Jones wasn't exactly in that category. But damn a man who whined. It was a trait that Longarm found tiresome.

"These handcuffs are bruising my wrists. Can't you loosen them?" Jones grumbled.

"I already loosened them all I dare," Longarm gritted around the cheroot that was clenched between his teeth. "Any more an' the damn things will fall off. Now gather your bag. This isn't a regular stop. They'll only pause long enough for you an' me to drop off on the platform. If there even is a platform here."

"I can't carry it with my hands manacled like this."

"You carried it this far," Longarm told him. "But I tell you what. If it's too much for you . . ."

"Yes?" Jones urged. He had a satisfied, victorious look about him now that he thought Longarm was going to offer to carry the Gladstone for him.

Longarm exhaled a thin stream of smoke. "You can always leave the son of a bitch behind. Somebody's bound t' find it and get some use out of the stuff in there."

Jones went into a sulk. A quiet one. Which Longarm did not mind in the slightest.

The conductor appeared at the front of the coach about the time the brakes began to squeal and the train commenced to slow.

"Your stop is just ahead, Marshal. Come this way, please."

Longarm got up and motioned Jones into the aisle ahead of him, then plucked his own carpetbag down from the rack overhead. He noticed that Jones was able to manage the Gladstone just fine. It was not a surprise. Did it without comment, too. Which was a surprise.

The three of them, the conductor in the lead, walked to the back of the car and onto the small steel platform there. Longarm held onto his carpetbag with one hand and the rail with the other. Jones, hampered by the handcuffs and unwilling to set his bag down, was thrown against the back wall of the passenger coach when the train lurched to a halt. He hit hard enough to make Longarm wince, but this time Jones said nothing. Still sulking, Longarm guessed. Now if only that mood would hold all the way back to Denver. . . .

"Be quick, please," the conductor said. "This is only a stop and go."

"Right."

Jones, with Longarm close behind him, descended the built-in-steps. They had to jump the last two feet to reach the wooden planking that passed for a platform here as there was no step-stool available like there would have been at a regular stop.

The conductor was already signaling ahead for the engineer to apply power again when Longarm thanked him. The man flashed a smile and a brief "You're welcome." By then it was difficult to hear over the sound of clashing couplings as the cars, which had been compressed close together by stopping, began to expand to the limits of the shackles once again when the locomotive accelerated.

Longarm turned to survey their surroundings. What he saw was not exactly promising.

There was no depot here. Just the flat platform, which did not even have a roof over it; a signal stand where train orders could be hung; and a tiny, weather-beaten telegraph shanty.

There was no sign of horses and not even a livestock chute or holding pen along the tracks. Not a wagon nor stagecoach and no indication of how—or if—the telegrapher arrived for work. There was nothing.

Jones looked nervous.

And the truth of the matter was that Longarm felt a twinge of apprehension himself. He did not know where the hell this Salt Springs place was or how they were supposed to get there.

"Well, shit," he said aloud, tossing the stub of his cheroot into the rock ballast under the train tracks.

# Chapter 14

"Hello? Is anyone here? Hello!" Longarm walked over to the lone window in the telegrapher's shack and peered in. He damn near jumped out of his skin when he saw a bearded apparition peering back at him.

The face looked like something out of a magazine line cut, perhaps illustrating an Edgar Allen Poe horror story.

The man was badly scarred. He had a long beard with food stains in it and wildly unkempt gray hair. His eyes were pale, rheumy and frightened.

"Hello," Longarm tried again. "Are you the telegraph operator here?"

"Who're you?" the man inside the shack replied in a thin, scratchy voice that he probably did not get to exercise very often.

Longarm introduced himself and gave Jones's name as well.

"What're you doing here?"

"We need transportation to Salt Springs. Could you tell us when the next coach will be along?"

"Huh! That's a good one."

"Did I say something funny?"

"Hell, yes. Don't no coaches come here. Not never. Never seen a coach here. None."

"I see wheel tracks over there," Longarm pointed out.

"Ayuh. Could be you do. Wa'n't no coach made them tracks though."

"All right, what did make them and when will it be back?"

"That's Clete Harkins's wagon made them an' Bobby Jessup's."

"Fine. When will one of them be back?"

The telegrapher dug a fingernail deep into his beard and scratched while he thought. "Clete, he might be along any day now. Depends on if he has any cheese t' ship. An' Bobby, he comes 'most every month or two t' pick up supplies and load those bags o' medicinal salts." The fellow snorted. "Medicinal. My ass, they're medicinal. Plain old salt off the flats, but Bobby has fancy ideas, see. Makes these little boxes an' dribbles in a little salt an' calls it something highfalutin and sells it all the way over to Europe, wherever th' hell that is. I dunno myself. Heard about it. Never been there."

"Europe, you mean."

"That's what I said, ain't it?"

"Yes. Of course, it is. Are these, uh, gentlemen residents of Salt Springs?"

"Nope. Not the both of them, they ain't. Cletus, he lives over yonder a piece." The fellow gestured vaguely toward the northeast where one of Nevada's countless small mountains lay only a few miles distant. "Now Bobby, he does live in Salt Springs. Only person that does, you see."

"The only . . ."

"Bobby, he's the one started the place. Come in here with grand ideas all the way back in, oh, the fifties sometime, I think it was. Afore the railroad came, I know that. Had big plans, I guess. Tried t' get the tracks to come up that way. Figured to make a fortune mining salt, y'see. Instead, they built plumb acrost the salt flats east o' here, which meant Bobby didn't have no big-time salt business. Some other fella is getting rich off salt, not Bobby. When all that happened, everybody cleared out of Salt Springs. All 'cept Bobby. He's still there. Drives down every once in a blue moon t' ship his little boxes and pick up mail, food, like that."

"What about the sheriff or the marshal or whoever the law is up there? I understand there's a lawman in Salt Springs."

"That'd be Bobby. He's also the mayor, town council, justice o' the peace, clerk o' court. Whoever you're looking for, Bobby is him."

"Jesus!" Longarm blurted.

"When is the next train east?" Jones asked. He had drifted over to listen in and was obviously ready to get back on the train and head for Denver without further delay.

"You shush," Longarm told him. He turned back to the telegraph operator. "How can we get to Salt Springs, friend? D'you have horses we could rent or a wagon? Anything?"

The fellow dug around inside his beard again for a minute or so, then said, "Clete might could take you."

"That would be Mr. Harkins?"

"Tha's right. Cletus Harkins. Lives over yonder."

"Yes, I believe we already established that. How do we contact your Mr. Harkins so we can get a ride in his wagon?"

"Just walk up to his door, I reckon, an' ask him."

"All right, fine. And how do we do that?"

"I already done tol' you that, mister. You walk up to his door. You know. Like you put one foot out an' then another one an' keep it up for a spell. Direc'ly you'll be at Clete's door. Then you ask him. No idea if he'll do it, though. I don't recall as anybody's ever wanted a ride to Salt Springs before. Don't know as Clete's ever been there his own self. But you can ask him. You surely can."

"This place of his . . ."

"'Bout four, five miles. Over that way. Jus' follow the wagon track. The one that bends off t' the east. The track goin' north is Bobby's. Goes t' Salt Springs. O' course you could walk that, too, but I wouldn't recommend it. But you do what you want."

"Be all right if we leave our bags here with you ?"

"Sure. Just set 'em down. Nobody's gonna come along and bother them, that's for damn sure."

Longarm looked at the sky. Then at the ground. He caught himself in time to avoid asking any stupid questions about rain or anything like that. It looked like it last rained in the vicinity along about the time of Noah's flood. And the country here only got a sprinkle that time.

"Thank you, friend. We're obliged. Come on, Jones."

"Me? I don't want to walk anywhere."

"All right then. Suit yourself." Longarm bent down to open his carpetbag and take out another pair of handcuffs.

"What are you doing? I've already got these on," Jones said.

"For your ankles. I can't carry you and you don't want to walk. I figure since I have to leave you here untended, I'll need to tighten the cuffs on your wrists and lock your legs around something. That telegraph post over there, I think. That looks like a good spot. Come along."

"But . . ."

"I don't expect to be more than a day or two," Longarm said. "Depending on how far it is. Don't just stand there now. Come along."

"I think . . . I changed my mind. I want to go with you to Salt Springs."

Longarm shrugged. "Whatever pleases you." He thought for a moment, then slipped the extra set of handcuffs into his coat pocket. He probably would need them when—if— he found Marshal/Mayor/Judge Bobby Jessup and Billy Vail's kin Edgar Bowman.

"Come along, Mr. Jones. We won't get anyplace standing around here." Longarm set off at a brisk pace and Jones, apparently deciding to make the best of the situation, jogged in broad circles to get a little running in while Longarm walked following the wagon tracks.

# Chapter 15

Cletus Harkins was a tall man with a wispy scrap of chin whiskers and a tic in his left eyebrow and another on his cheek. It made it difficult to look him in the eye without staring at the tics.

He was, however, quite welcoming.

"Yeah, you can hire my mules and wagon. Ten dollars a day. Two dollars extra if you don't got your own feed for them."

"Twelve dollars a day!" Longarm blurted. "That's outrageous. I can hire a wagon for a week for that money and a driver to go with it."

"Fine with me, mister. Go hire him then."

"How far is it up to Salt Springs?"

"Don't know. Never been there." Harkins pulled a rather grubby plug of tobacco from his back pocket and gnawed a corner off of it, then stuck the plug back into his pocket without offering it to his guests.

"We'll take the wagon then," Longarm said.

"Uh huh. Thought you would."

"I don't suppose your missus could fix us up a box lunch to carry along on the trip."

"Reckon she could. That'd be a dollar extra. For each of youse."

"Why am I not surprised to hear you say that?" Longarm mumbled.

"You don't want the lunches?"

"We want the lunches. And the wagon. And the feed."

"You'd be going to Salt Springs?"

"That's right."

"Two days then. You can pay in advance."

Longarm did not like it. Did not like Harkins very much either. But he did not see that they had a whole hell of a lot of choice about it. And he knew full well this gray and dour man would not accept any government voucher for his payment. Longarm dug deep into his britches to come up with some gold coins to cover the rental and the meals. Dammit.

The wagon, when Harkins rolled it out, was no better than he might have expected. The wood was dried out and warped by the dry heat of this arid, barren country. In Denver he could have bought the damn thing for less than Harkins's rental fee. Including the mules. Well, all right. Maybe not the mules, too. They weren't so bad even if they were a bit on the small side for serious pulling. But the wagon was ready to be broken apart and the running gear salvaged.

Longarm carefully inspected the wheels and rims before he accepted the rig. He had no idea how rough the country was ahead, and the prospect of a broken wheel was not pleasant. Fortunately the spokes were tight and strong and the iron tires were well-fitted. Harkins threw a pair of spare wheels into the box anyway and loaded in some grass hay and a sack of four gallons or so of mixed grains, barley

76

and oats and a little corn. But then he would need to have feed on hand for the flock of goats Longarm could see inside a large pen close to the man's ramshackle house.

The house looked to be in need of some repairs, but the barn and pens were in as good a condition as the wagon wheels. Apparently, Cletus Harkins was a man who held to his priorities.

Harkins delivered a poke containing some chunks of unidentified fried meat that could have been antelope but was probably kid, a dozen cold biscuits, two huge chunks of pale cheese, about two fingers of lard wrapped in a twist of greasy paper and a rather heavy tin with a screw top.

"I'll thank you to bring that water can back with you. Be wanting to use it again sometime."

"Yes, we'll do that, thanks."

"And have the wagon back no later than the day after tomorrow. I got a load of grain coming in on the train then and I don't want to leave it setting on the platform over there."

"We'll be back just as quick as we can."

"All right then."

Longarm climbed onto the driving box beside Jones, who was already sitting there looking like he would rather be almost anyplace on earth than this godforsaken little goat farm in the middle of nowhere.

"Hiyup, mules. Git along." He shook the driving lines to rattle the bits and get the critters's attention, and the pair of big-eared, rat-tailed, cat-hammed little mules set off at a spanking trot.

# Chapter 16

Longarm had thought Clete Harkins's farm was in the middle of nowhere. Well, Salt Springs was exactly square in the center of damn nowhere then. Except there was more of it. An entire, if small, town of sun-baked board and batten structures arranged along two sides of a wide spot that passed for the main—and only—street.

"Makes you wonder what would keep folks living in a place like this, doesn't it?" Jones observed, reaching up to scratch his nose. Longarm had long since removed the handcuffs. After all, where could he run to out here regardless of how fast he could scamper.

Longarm looked around. Everything in sight, land and sky and buildings alike, looked like they had been bleached of color by the constant glare of the sun. Even the low, north-south lying mountains visible some miles distant were pale, all rugged gray rock with neither grass nor tree apparent from down on the flat.

And the flat here was genuinely, truly, depressingly flat. Billiard tables could take lessons from the ground here.

Except for one pile of white earth that could be seen on the far side of town. That exception was as tall as the buildings close to it.

As they drove nearer to the town Longarm saw there was another terrain feature that he hadn't noticed at first, perhaps because the angle of the sinking sun did not reflect in their direction. The land beyond Salt Springs wasn't land at all but water. A vast sheet of shallow water that must have encompassed hundreds, perhaps thousands of acres. Salt Springs seemed to have been built on the edge of a huge lake.

No, he thought as they drove still closer, it wasn't really a lake. More like the world's biggest puddle. Strange.

Longarm drove up to the livery barn on the edge of town and stepped down. "Hello. Is anybody here?"

The place seemed deserted save for a pair of small, furry-eared burros, both of them in the same stall.

"Hello?" he tried again.

"I don't see anybody," Jones said from the doorway leading into the tack room. "Don't see any equipment, either. No saddles or harness or anything at all except for two blankets and some rope."

"Nothing?"

"Look for yourself if you don't believe me."

"No need to get on your high horse. I believe you. It's just . . . odd. You know?"

"Yes, it is."

"Well, odd or not and, with or without a hostler, we're gonna take these mules outa their riggin' and put them in those stalls over there. Then we'll go see if we can't find this Bobby Jessup. Give me a hand, will you?"

Ten minutes later, with the mules contently enjoying hay and a bit of the grain Harkins had packed for them,

Longarm and Jones walked over to the town marshal's office, conveniently identified by a sign over the door.

"Hello?" Longarm tapped on the door and, hearing no answer, tried the knob. The door was not locked. But then, he discovered, there was no need to bother locking it for there was nothing inside that could be stolen. Nothing save a rather large desk and one of the steel cages that were sold already welded and shipped unassembled to jails all over the west. The cell was empty, its door standing open.

"The place is deserted," Jones said.

"Jessup is supposed to be here someplace. And a man named Bowman. Makes you wonder what happened to everybody else though, doesn't it?"

"Not me. I'd leave too if some horrid mistake brought me here. I would leave just as quickly as I could and not look back."

"We'll try the other places. They have to be somewhere, dammit."

The mercantile, the saloon and the barbershop were empty shells that looked like no one had set foot inside them in months, perhaps years. Even the bar had been hauled away from the saloon although a pale outline on the floor showed where it once stood. Longarm and Jones were walking down the center of the street when they heard a thump from behind the buildings ahead of them.

"There." Longarm extended his stride now that he finally had a direction in which to look. "That has to be them."

They emerged from the alley between two abandoned buildings to find two men with shovels laboring beside the pile of dirt Longarm had noticed before.

Both men were bearded and disheveled and were bare to the waist and barefoot, standing knee deep in water as they lifted heavy wet earth from the bottom of the sump or well or whatever the hell it was they were digging here. Both were skinny to the point of emaciation, ribs and collarbones prominent. Both were gray-haired. And both looked very annoyed with the distraction of being disturbed at their labors.

"This is private property. Go away," the one with the longer beard said when he saw the intruders. "Go away or I'll charge you with trespass."

"That would make you Jessup, wouldn't it? And that means you would be Bowman," Longarm said to the other man. "I'm a deputy United States marshal and I've come to take you home."

"No!" Edgar Bowman cried. He turned and tried to run, slipping and sliding in the water and, after a moment, sprawling face down in it.

Longarm considered with distaste the idea of going in after him, then decided to wait a bit rather than get his boots and pant legs wet. Edgar could not really run away. There was nowhere for him to go and no place for him to hide, the poor, sad, hopeless lunatic.

# Chapter 17

"Can't we just forget this whole thing?" It was Bobby Jessup who asked the question. It was late in the afternoon and the four of them were seated around a table in the building that used to be a café, each with a cup of . . . water. Jessup could not afford such fripperies as coffee or tea.

"Forgive me, Ed," Jessup continued. "I sent that note shortly after you got here." To Longarm and Jones he said, "Ed was very open with me from the first day. He told me who he was and where he came from. He said he wanted a place to hide. I . . . I said he could stay. Then I wrote that note to his family. He even told me where they lived. I am ashamed to admit it, but I hoped there would be a reward for his capture. Then I came to know him and came to deeply regret telling anyone where he was."

"At least it was Pip you told and not those people at the asylum," Bowman said.

"Pip?" Longarm raised an eyebrow.

"Oh." Bowman actually blushed a little. At least Longarm was fairly sure it was a blush he saw beneath the man's dry, sun-darkened skin. "Pip is what I've always called my cousin. And I am Pug." He laughed. "Or sometimes Poop when she would be annoyed with me and no one else was around to hear. I don't remember how those names got started, but we've always used them and still do." Bowman sighed. "I really do love her. I'm sorry to have worried her."

"She still loves you as well, Ed," Longarm said. "Despite . . . you know." He kept surreptitiously peering at Ed Bowman, looking for signs of the man's lunacy. So far he was hiding it awfully well, though.

But then, Longarm supposed, mental instability was not something that would necessarily show on the outside and could probably take many forms, some of which might be thought of as simply innocent quirkiness unless you knew better. Ed Bowman's craziness was probably one of those types that was not immediately apparent. In any event, finding him to be lucid, even pleasant, was a very nice surprise.

"I need for Ed to stay here, Marshal," Bobby Jessup put in. "He's helping me on a new project. Ed is a fine engineer, you see, and I have plans that really need his services."

"What would that be?" Longarm asked, reaching for another very small helping of the tepid water, which he learned had to be hauled from a spring at the base of one of the small mountains some seven miles away. You did not want to waste any drinking water when it was so hard to come by.

"You probably already heard that the railroad's choice of route ruined my plan to capture the salt market in this continent. The town blossomed when I started the business and then died just as quickly when the railroad announced their route—although the route I anticipated would have been much, much better. Anyway, since then, I've barely been able to stay alive by selling my medicinal salts in Europe and India. For some reason, they are fairly popular among the British officers' wives in India.

"As soon as my new project takes shape though, Marshal, my customers will be disappointed for I expect to stop selling the salts and concentrate on salmon, instead."

"Salmon?" Longarm asked.

"Yes, exactly. It occurred to me that I have all this salt-infused water available. I should make use of it. So what I intend to do is to build a sequence of ponds with the saltwater flowing in one, then continuing on through many others and finally out the other side, you see."

"All right, but why?"

Jessup beamed. "I intend to raise salmon in those ponds."

"Tame salmon?"

"So to speak, yes. I will start then as hatchlings at different times so they don't all mature at the same time, then as they come of age to harvest, I can sell fresh fish as far away as Virginia City and Ogden, perhaps even as far as Cheyenne and Denver. Think of it. People love smoked salmon. How much more will they pay for fresh salmon?"

"Where will the roe come from?" Jones asked.

"What's roe?"

"The eggs. Fish eggs are called roe."

Jessup shrugged. "I didn't know that. Anyway, I intend to buy some. I'm sure it can be arranged. And once I get started, I can simply breed them here."

"Salmon breed in freshwater. They live in saltwater most of their lives, but they breed and then they die in fresh," Jones said.

"Really?"

"Yes, really."

"Did you know that, Ed?"

"I don't know anything about fish, Bobby. I told you that to begin with. I can create your ponds and the water-handling structures, but I don't know a thing about fish. Don't even like to eat them."

"Damn," Jessup said. Then he shrugged again. "Perhaps I will have to raise a different fish then. Or oys—no, you can already buy oysters packed in ice and shipped by rail." He snapped his fingers. "I have it. Lobster, that's it. I shall pond-raise lobsters." He gave Jones a slightly worried look. "Lobsters don't breed in freshwater, do they?"

"Uh, not as far as I ever heard."

"Good. Then I will raise lobsters instead of salmon. Either way, I need Ed's help to design everything."

Longarm was not entirely sure which one of them at this table was the lunatic. But all he said was, "Edgar, I hope you will come with me willingly."

"To see Pip, you say, not to . . . that other place."

"That's right. She wants to bring you home. She's terribly worried about you. She wants to see you. She and Billy couldn't come right away and they didn't want to delay getting you home, and I was traveling nearby anyway to, uh, escort Mr. Jones back to Denver. I promised I would see you safely back."

"Don't go, Ed. Please. I need you here."

"You're very kind, Bobby, but . . . Pip is very special to me. She has been for my entire life. If she wants me . . . will they put me in another asylum there, do you think?"

"I don't know about that," Longarm lied. "All I'm sure of is that she is desperately worried. She wants to see you more than anything in the world right now."

"Bobby, I'm sorry, but family has to come first. You can understand that, can't you?"

"Damn it, Ed, you promised."

"I did no such thing. Besides, you tried to sell me in exchange for some reward money. I'm just lucky it was my cousin I told you about and not that . . . place."

"I didn't mean . . . well, that was before I got to know you. And I already said I was sorry, didn't I?"

"Yes, but I have to go with the marshal and his friend."

"You'll come back and help me finish my project, won't you? Together we can revolutionize the marketing of fish in this country. Lobster, I mean." He giggled. "I forgot. It's lobster now, isn't it? We'll completely modernize the raising and sale of lobsters, Ed. The two of us. We can do it. Partners, fair and square, everything split right down the middle."

"I'll think about it, Bobby, but first I'll go to Denver with the marshal and have a visit with my cousin. Marshal, are you *sure* she won't said me back to . . . you know?"

"That I can promise you," Longarm said. "They do not intend to send you back to that place." He saw no point in mentioning that they already found a lunatic asylum in Georgetown that would accept Edgar Bowman as a . . . what the hell were crazies called in such places anyway? Patient? Guest? Or just inmate, which was what they really were anyway.

Whatever he would be called there, at least he would be close to people who loved him. And wouldn't Billy's wife be pleased to know that he still knew and loved her, too.

This was going to work out very nicely, Longarm thought. Very nicely, indeed.

"We'll start back in the morning," he said.

"Couldn't you stay a little while? A few days, that's all," Jessup whined. "If we all four work, why, we can accomplish ever so much on the ponds."

"In the morning," Longarm repeated.

# Chapter 18

Longarm drove the wagon back to the railroad depot and the hell with Clete Harkins. He had already paid the man for the use of the rig, and Longarm was in no mood to be walking from the farm back to the depot. Besides, he did not know the train schedule here and did not want to miss the next eastbound coming through. Let Harkins walk to reclaim his property.

As they came near to the tracks Longarm slowed the wagon almost to a halt and motioned for Bowman and Jones to lean closer. "Boys, I want you both to understand something. We're prob'ly just fine here. Take us a nice little train ride. Have a few beers and a good meal or two. Then get back to Denver and take care of whatever business is waiting for each of us. But back in Fannin we had us that bit of trouble." He looked at Bowman. "Did Jones tell you about that, Ed?"

"Yes, he did. He said some people tried to kill him."

"It was just the one man that time, but you never know if the people behind it will try again. So I want the two of you t' help me out. Just in case there's another assassination attempt, you see. I want to be unencumbered and free to fight back without worrying about what you two are up to.

"Now I know you've both agreed to cooperate, and I truly appreciate that. I'm counting on it, in fact. But rules are rules and I'd best follow them." He grinned. "Most of the time anyway. The point is, seeing as neither one of you is really under arrest, just in protective custody, I got to be extra special careful to watch out for your welfare.

"So what I want t' do is to handcuff you . . . don't give me that hangdog look now, dammit, there are rules about this . . . what I want t' do is handcuff you to each other. That leaves me free to jump if anybody comes after us. Free t' do whatever has t' be done, see.

"While I'm doing all that, I want each o' you t' watch out for the other. I want you to cooperate, like. In return I'll let you have as much freedom of movement as I reasonably can since I can be pretty sure neither of you will try and jump off the train while you're chained to somebody else or do anything stupid like that. You can move around some on the train without me having to circle around like some damn buzzard looking for trouble."

"What about my runs?" Jones asked. "Ed can't keep up with me when I run." He was still breathing hard from running beside the wagon much of the way down from Salt Springs.

"We're gonna be on a train, Jones. If you tell me you can run alongside a railroad train an' keep up with it I'll get to thinking you're a liar, and you wouldn't like that, for if I think you're a liar, then I'll think I can't trust you t' move around unsupervised."

"What if someone starts shooting?" Bowman asked.

"All I want you two t' do in that case is to get the hell

outta the way. Drop down to the ground or jump behind something. I'll handle everything else an' it will be a big help t' me knowing I don't have t' be worrying about what you're up to. I can concentrate on the shooter."

Ed Bowman looked away for a moment, his eyes unfocused as he gave thought to something. Whatever it was, he quickly squared his shoulders and said, "Before you chain us, could I go inside the telegrapher's shack alone for a few minutes? I want . . . just in case something should happen before we get to Denver, I want to let Pip know that I am all right and that . . . I love her. Would that be all right?"

"Sure. Are you gonna send her a wire?"

Bowman nodded.

"D'you have any money to pay for it?"

The man blushed beneath his thick beard and bright sunburn. "No, I . . . I hadn't thought about that."

Longarm reached into his pocket. "Here. This should cover it. An' while you're in there, find out when the next train is due, will you? I don't know all that much about such things but I think the operator will have to send train orders to the next station telling the eastbound that they have passengers to pick up here for a change. I wouldn't expect they'd generally stop here."

"Thanks."

Longarm brought the wagon to a halt beside the depot and got down to tend to the mules while Bowman went inside to send his telegram. Tomlin Jones looked for a patch of shade to get away from the weight of the burning afternoon sun.

Longarm also unloaded a pile of the so-called medicinal salts—medicinal in a pig's eye, but it seemed that people who had too much money would buy just any damn thing; he had agreed to bring the salts down to the railroad for Bobby Jessup, saving the odd hermit and his burros a trip.

This deal wasn't turning out to be so bad, he thought as he stripped the harness off Harkins's mules. Both Jones and Bowman were being cooperative, and the eastbound would be along by-and-by. Just another day or so and they would all be comfortably back in Denver to go their own ways.

That is what he was thinking at the time.

But then he had been wrong once or twice before.

# Chapter 19

"Evanston. Evanston, Wyoming Territory. Next stop, Evanston." The conductor walked the length of car in a rolling, seafarer's gait, seeming to hardly even notice the swaying and bumping of the passenger coach.

Longarm pulled out his Ingersol and checked the time. "Y'know something? I haven't had a decent rest in days and we aren't gonna get one on a Union Pacific train. I think we'll get off here an' spend the night in a proper hotel for a change. We can take the first eastbound tomorrow an' let the government treat us to a good meal and a comfortable bed in the meantime. Any objections?"

"Certainly not from me," Jones said. "I am in no great hurry now, and the thought of a good meal is enticing."

"You, Ed?" Longarm asked.

"Oh, I will go along with whatever the two of you prefer." A hesitant smile tickled the corners of his lips. "Whatever."

"That settles it then."

"What about our tickets?" Jones asked.

"You and I are traveling on my badge. It don't matter a whit to us. An' Ed's ticket will allow a layover if he wants."

"Then I say we should get off now."

The brakes began to squeal and the train to clatter as the cars rattled together approaching the platform in Evanston. Longarm and Jones stood and retrieved their bags from the overhead rack. Ed Bowman had no luggage to worry about but was forced to stand also since he was handcuffed to Tomlin Jones's right wrist.

Apparently Bowman had escaped from the asylum back in Utah with nothing but the clothing on his back. Longarm had not tried to press him for information about that. For one thing, it might have been painful to the man. For another, it was none of Custis Long's damned business. All he was doing here was performing a favor for two people he cared about very much, and if they wanted Bowman brought to Denver, then brought to Denver he would be.

Three other people in the coach also stood and collected their things, bracing themselves against the movement of the train as they did so: a middle-aged couple who had been sitting on the other side of the car and a nicely dressed gentleman in the back. All were prepared by the time the train clanked and hissed to a stop.

"Evanston. All out for Evanston," the conductor intoned as he made his way forward again. "All out for Evanston, Wyoming Territory."

"All together now," Longarm said and warned, "don't try an' run or I'll cut the legs out from under one o' you. I'll leave it to you boys to think about which one I'll put the bullet into."

Not that he expected any such thing would happen. Not really. Jones could certainly outrun him . . . but not with Ed Bowman dangling off his arm like a fancy woman's bangle. Longarm did not think he had to worry about any escape attempts and likely wouldn't have to even if the men had not been handcuffed. Which did not mean he could abandon caution. He would keep the cuffs on most of the time and be safe rather than risk being sorry.

The three let the lady and her husband disembark first, then followed them down onto the platform. The businessman was the last to get off and he immediately set off down the street while the couple walked back toward the baggage car.

"Where are we going?" Bowman asked.

"There's a hotel down the block. I've stayed there before," Longarm said.

Jones sniffed. "I know the place. It is a fleabag. Quite unacceptable."

"Do you know anything better?" Longarm challenged.

"Anything would be better. But in answer to your question, yes. I know a very nice little place. They cater to a select clientele. I stayed there many times when I was working for Mr. Staley."

"D'you think they'll give you a room now that you aren't working for the big man?"

"They will if they know what is good for them. I could say a thing or two about their billing practices if I wanted to."

Jones did not elaborate on the comment and Longarm did not ask him to. But he tucked the information away to pass along to the United States attorney when they got back to Denver.

"Lead the way then," Longarm said.

Jones set out at a swift pace, Bowman struggling to keep up at his side and Longarm striding along behind.

He was looking forward to a good meal, a fine cigar and a restful night's sleep in a comfortable bed.

# Chapter 20

The meal was superb, the cigar excellent and the night's sleep . . . crowded. The room was large enough and very nicely furnished but it nonetheless had only one bed in it, and Longarm had himself and the two prisoners to bed down.

Jones was already in a snit because Longarm would not spend the government's money on a twelve-dollar bottle of brandy for the SOB. Twelve damn dollars; that was two week's pay for an ordinary man. And he started complaining about the sleeping arrangements even before Longarm announced them.

Ed Bowman volunteered to sleep on a pallet on the floor and said it would be a luxury at that.

"What the hell've you been used to?" Longarm asked.

Bowman shrugged. "It wasn't at all bad in Salt Springs, but at the . . . the . . . that place we had wood platforms. No mattress or blanket or anything. So if I could just wad up that extra blanket to sleep on, why, it would be fine."

Instead Longarm laid out the blanket for himself, placing it across the foot of the door so no one could get in or out without waking him. That let him take the handcuffs off his two charges so they could be comfortable while they slept. For his comfort, too, of course, as it kept Jones's whining down to the level of a mild grumble.

That was all right, and, like Ed Bowman, he had slept in much less comfortable situations. But in the morning, he started off the new day annoyed because with his prisoners in tow he couldn't even have a morning shit by himself. He had to take them with him to the backhouse and all of them had to stand aside pretending not to notice while one by one they took turns on the seat. Jones complained about that, too, but that time Longarm did not blame the man for his grousing.

"All right, everybody done here?" Longarm asked, not bothering to wait for their responses. "We'll go back upstairs and wash up in our room, then downstairs for breakfast. We have plenty of time before the next train east. It's only, what, eight or ten paces over to the back porch? I'm not gonna put the 'cuffs back on you yet. But don't either one of you so much as damn think about running. D'you hear?" This time he did stand there waiting until each man nodded.

"All right then. You fellas go first. I'll be right behind you. Straight for the steps and inside, and no lollygagging. Go on now."

The spring on the backhouse door creaked loud enough to wake the dead, and Ed Bowman took the lead stepping outside.

Almost immediately a fist-sized plug of wood was gouged out of the plank door and Jones grunted in pain, then fell to the ground writhing.

A moment later Longarm heard the crack of the rifle shot.

Longarm leaped forward and grabbed Ed Bowman by the arm and dragged him back inside the shitter. He bent and scooped Jones up, big as the man was, and threw him in behind Bowman.

"Stay here. Whatever happens, the two of you stay here where you can't be seen. You hear me? Don't neither one o' you move an inch from outta this spot."

He did not wait for answers that time either but, crouching, launched himself out of the backhouse, hit the ground rolling and extended his Colt in the general direction that the shot had come from.

It was just coming dawn and the town was mostly in deep shadow, and, for once, that worked to Longarm's advantage. When the rifleman fired again Longarm was able to clearly see the bright yellow flare of his muzzle flash, telling him exactly where the assassin was hiding.

He was standing behind a haphazardly stacked pile of fruit crates, using them to steady his aim. The gunner was in an alley on the other side of the street beside the hotel, shooting from a distance of perhaps sixty yards away. That would have been a good enough choice of ambush positions if the asshole could shoot worth sour apples.

Fortunately for Longarm, the rifleman was close enough for Longarm to return fire even though he only had his Colt. Bad shot or not, Longarm wasn't willing to let the rifleman get off any more rounds without being challenged.

Longarm cocked his revolver and took careful aim, then gently squeezed the trigger.

He did not aim at the top of the crates where the muzzle flash had been but in the center of them, figuring the light slats of a fruit crate would certainly not stop his bullet and probably would not even deflect it.

The big Colt bucked in his hand and, for a moment, he was blinded by his own muzzle flash.

He heard the report of the gunshot and was able to make out the answering flare of gunpowder from that alley across the street, but he had no idea where the slug went.

He heard a cry of pain that could well have been faked.

Then . . . nothing. Nothing except some muted whimpering coming from inside the hotel backhouse where Jones and Bowman were hunkered down.

No one from the hotel or in the street moved either. Sensible folks, Longarm thought. Gunfights make for a truly lousy spectator sport, after all, there being such a thin line between spectator and unwilling participant once lead begins flying.

Longarm waited long enough to decide the assassin was done, at least for the time being, and then waited a while longer.

By then he had to take a piss again and he was getting mighty damned tired of lying on the ground waiting for someone to try and kill him.

He waited until pale dawn turned to daylight bright enough let him clearly see if a head or a rifle barrel should pop into view from behind those crates.

Then, warily, he stood, Colt held ready.

"You boys stay where you are," he said to the closed door. "I'll be back in a minute. Just don't go no place until I come back for you. You hear me?"

Again he did not wait for an answer but began advancing—very carefully—across the street and into the alley where the unknown man with the rifle had been waiting for Tomlin Jones to emerge from that shitter.

# Chapter 21

The son of a bitch was not going to be answering any questions. He was lying in a mud puddle created by his own life's blood pouring out onto the ground. By the time Longarm got there he was stone dead and stank of the shit that filled his pants, ejected in his death throes the way so many of them often did.

Longarm wrinkled his nose, then went back to get Jones and Bowman.

"Is it safe?" Jones wanted to know.

"It's safe. He's dead."

"You shot him?"

"Yeah. Either my bullet deflected, which I didn't think it would do, or he was crouching down. However it happened, the slug passed along the side of his neck and tore out that big artery that runs there. He's dead."

"What if there is another one?"

"Then I'll shoot that one, too. Hopefully not so bad that I can't talk to him for a couple minutes before he dies. In fact, it could be a real good thing for another one to take a shot at you, Jones."

"Don't *say* something like that," Jones cried. "They might."

"We'll cross that bridge if and when we come to it. Right now I want you to take a look at him, see if you recognize him."

"Do I have to?"

"Yes, damn it, you have to. Now hold out your wrist. You too, Ed."

"But I don't want . . ."

Longarm's voice turned hard. "Do it."

Jones sighed, obviously thinking himself the most put-upon man in Christendom. But he held out his wrist next to Ed Bowman's, which was already obediently extended, and Longarm snapped the handcuffs on before he led them across the side street.

By that time, a few people had begun to emerge from the nearby buildings, and from the direction of the main street Longarm could see a tall, slender man wearing a policeman's dark, copper-buttoned jacket coming at a brisk walk.

"Hold it right there, you!" the cop ordered when he was thirty or so feet away.

It was Longarm's turn to sigh. The fellow did not even have his revolver out. Worse, it was carried awkwardly in a deep holster with a leather strap locking it firmly in place. Longarm figured the gun could be brought into action in, oh, two minutes or maybe a little less. But then, maybe the cop thought the pretty coat and the ducky little billed cap with the badge pinned on the front of it made him bulletproof. Damn thing would make him a better target in some quarters. Which this poor fellow seemed honestly not to know.

Longarm pulled out his wallet, his hand deliberately moving close to the grips of his coat just to see if that prompted any caution, but the tall policeman never seemed to notice, telling Longarm quite a lot about the fellow's competence. And common sense or lack thereof.

"Deputy United States marshal," Longarm announced, showing his badge and slipping it back into his pocket before the cop could get a good look at it. True to what Longarm expected, the man did not ask to examine the badge closely to see if it might be a fake. Longarm just hoped for the sake of the folks who lived here this man was not representative of their police force.

"Someone said they heard gunshots over here."

"I'm not surprised," Longarm said. "Guy over there tried to ambush me an' my prisoners."

"He shot at you?" the cop seemed quite shocked by that notion.

"Yes, an' I shot back. You'll find him lying over there in the alley. Behind those apple crates."

"You hit him?"

"I said I shot at him, didn't I? Of course I hit him."

"Is he . . . ?"

"Dead as a squashed bug."

They walked into the alley, trailed by half a dozen or so townspeople and a few guests from the hotel, one of whom Longarm recognized from the train the day before.

"Oh, Jesus!" the policeman blurted when he saw—and smelled—the very messy body lying there in shit and blood and piss. The cop bent double and deposited his breakfast onto the ground.

The sight and smell of that prompted Tomlin Jones to do the same. And Ed Bowman began to look so pale Longarm was afraid he was going to faint and fall right on top of the freshly deposited puke.

Longarm guided him and Jones to one side and sat them down on some broken nail kegs at the side of the alley. It was a good thing the dead man had not been hiding behind those or a bullet would not so easily have passed through.

"I know this man," the policeman said when he got control of his stomach and took a closer look.

"Local fella?" Longarm asked.

"Yes. His name is Larry. I don't know his last name. He's a layabout and a troublemaker. Was, I should say. He won't be causing any more trouble now. He hangs a-round . . . hung around, I suppose . . . the Brass Lantern. That is a billiards parlor and, um, recreation spot frequented by railroadmen and the lower sort among our townspeople."

"Recreation spot," Longarm repeated.

"There are, well . . ." The cop actually blushed. "They are, uh . . ."

"You're trying to tell me there are whores there, right?"

"Um, yes. I suppose so."

"You suppose so? You don't know? You don't know that having a few whores on a string is the best source of information a lawman can have? Good Lord, man!"

The cop did not respond to that. Longarm was just glad he did not have to depend on this man to back him up. Now that would be a scary thought.

"Help me drag him over there where there isn't so much crap on the ground," Longarm said.

"Why?"

"Just do it. Please. Take that arm an' I'll take this one.

Good. Now we'll pull the bastard over there an' up onto those produce crates. They look sturdy enough t' hold his weight."

"Why do you . . . ?"

"I have to go through his pockets, don't I?"

"Do you?"

"Mister . . ." Longarm abso-damn-lutely refused to call this fool *officer*. "You tell me he's local. Me and my prisoners aren't. We're just passing through. Stopped to get some food and sleep an' that's all. So this Larry fella had no reason to be lying in an alley with that rifle over there waiting to shoot one of us. If he didn't have a reason of his own, then somebody gave him one. He was hired for the job. I want to see if there's a note or anything in his pockets that will tell me who it was that hired him. Now why don't you pick that rifle up before someone decides he wants it?"

"But it's all . . . dirty."

"Yes, it is. It's bloody as hell. But you know what? Blood washes off real fine. Now get the fucking rifle, will you?"

"Yes, sir." The cop seemed much more comfortable following orders than doing anything difficult. Like thinking. He stepped into the mud, slipped just a little, and reached down to use two fingers to very, very gingerly pluck the .45-60 caliber Kennedy repeater out of the gore.

"Now what?"

Longarm ignored him, concentrating on the dead man.

He did not really expect to learn anything, but he had to try. And with no real expectation of success, he was not especially disappointed when the man's pockets revealed nothing more than a bandana, a clasp knife, a dollar and twelve cents in silver . . . and one hundred fifty dollars in bright and shiny gold coins.

That would have been a down payment, Longarm figured, with at least that much again to be paid upon completion of the job.

One quick, well-aimed shot and slip away and he would be three hundred dollars richer. Maybe more.

Except that first shot had not been particularly well aimed in the half-light of dawn.

And you only get one shot free for nothing. All others have to be earned the hard way. It was a deadly game Longarm had played all too often before.

Worse, since this dead asshole was so very obviously a tool and not the root cause of the assassination attempt; there could very well be more coming between here and home.

All of a sudden Denver seemed very far away.

Longarm jerked his head around in alarm to check on his prisoners but Tomlin Jones and Ed Bowman were both sitting patiently where he had planted them.

"Take care o' this mess, will you?" Longarm said to the policeman.

"I'll need . . . there are reports to fill out. I'll need you to write something out and sign it. And there will have to be a coroner's inquest. You will have to make an appearance then. Are you staying at the hotel?"

"Yes," Longarm said. And it was, technically speaking, the truth.

Of course, the rest of that truth was that they would be at the hotel long enough to wash up, have breakfast and get their things together.

After that, the three of them would be back on an eastbound passenger coach, headed for Denver, Colorado. There was no damn way he intended hanging around here signing papers while some unknown son of a bitch arranged for a second—or was that third, considering the shooting incident back in Fannin?—attempt on their lives.

"I will get the paperwork started and bring everything to you later. Or do you want to come to city hall instead?"

"Oh, I'll come to city hall. Take care of the body, then wait for me t' join you there," Longarm said.

It'd be one hell of a long wait. But then the cop did not have to be told that. Surely he would figure it out for himself. Eventually.

"Come along," Longarm said to Jones and Bowman. They pushed through the still growing crowd and returned to the hotel.

# Chapter 22

"Well, shit," Longarm grumbled.

"What's wrong?"

"Oh, there's a break in the rails somewhere up ahead. A bridge or something like that. So they're having to take everyone around it in coaches. The detour takes forever, and it's bumpy and the food is lousy and . . . and I just don't damn well like it. That's what's wrong."

"I'm sorry I asked," Bowman said.

Jones scowled but said nothing. He had been largely quiet ever since they boarded the train that morning. Scared was Longarm's guess. There had been two attempts on his life since Longarm got him out of that jail back in Nevada, and no one stays lucky forever. Not even deputy United States marshals. Tomlin Jones was certainly bright enough to figure that out.

The conductor came through the cars explaining and apologizing while the train continued to slow out here in the middle of nowhere. Longarm was already on his feet collecting his bag. He handed Jones's Gladstone down to him while he was at it.

"I have to take a crap," Jones complained.

"Jeez! Why didn't you think about that before?" Longarm groaned.

"Because I didn't know we had to get off, that's why."

"Okay, fine, but be damned quick about it. Leave your bag on the seat. And hurry the hell back."

"What about these handcuffs?"

"What about them?" Longarm countered.

"I don't want to . . . you know . . . with him standing right there."

"Then hold it."

Jones flushed a dark red. "That's what I have been doing," he admitted. "I can't keep it in any longer."

"Good Lord," Longarm said. "Go on. Hurry."

"What about . . . you know . . . wiping?"

"Jones, get your ass down there an' do what you got t' do an' get the hell back here. Right now. Or I won't be lettin' you go at all. And stop all your bellyaching. I'm sure Ed doesn't want t' be chained to you any more 'n you want t' be with him. Now get the hell down there or forget about it."

Jones scurried down the aisle, practically dragging Ed Bowman with him, while the other passengers gathered themselves for departure.

The train came to a hissing, clanking halt and people began filing out of the two passenger cars. By the time Jones and Bowman emerged from the shitter down at the end of the coach, they and Longarm were the last passengers left aboard except for a very pretty girl who was burdened with about two too many hat boxes and was having trouble getting everything together.

"Would you allow me to help you, miss?" Ed Bowman offered.

She looked at him, saw the handcuffs connecting him to a glowering Tomlin Jones and blinked.

Smiling and undaunted, Bowman said, "I do have one hand free, and I'd be pleased to help you."

The girl looked at Longarm. "Are you . . . are they . . . ?"

"I'm a deputy marshal, miss. United States deputy. An' neither o' these men would harm you. They're both in protective custody is all. They aren't violent criminals or nothing like that."

"I see, and . . ."

"Why don't you let the gent take that heavy bag for you, an' I can carry one o' your hat boxes. You should be able t' manage the little travel case an' the other box, shouldn't you?"

"Yes, I . . . that would be very nice of you, uh, gentlemen." Her smile was a little nervous. But she did manage to smile at Ed when he lifted the larger of her bags from her hand.

"C'mon now, folks," Longarm said. "We're all bound t' be in the last coach as it is, an' we sure don't want t' miss it altogether."

The girl—damn but she was a looker—led the way off the coach with Bowman and Jones close behind and Longarm bringing up the rear. Which was just fine by him as it gave him ample opportunity to admire the view of the pretty, dark-haired little gal with the hat boxes.

# Chapter 23

"I am Miss Sally Ann Prindle of Baltimore . . . Baltimore
is in Maryland, you know . . . and I have been having the
most absolutely *mar*velous time out here in the wicked,
wicked West. Why, do you know what I heard today? I
overheard a gentleman speak of a duel to the very death
that occurred in Evanston . . . Evanston is one of those dry,
dreary little towns back there somewhere I believe . . . but
my point is, this very morning two gentlemen engaged in a
duel . . . with guns . . . and now one of them is dead. And I
suppose the other shall be soon enough. They will hang
him, you know. By the neck until he is dead. Oh, hanging is
such a horrible thing. I witnessed a hanging while I was
visiting my chum Cynthia . . . that is what I was doing out
here, you know, visiting . . . in any event, I did observe a
hanging, and it was a most terrible thing to behold. It
makes me shudder to think about it now." And by way of
demonstration, she shuddered. Visibly.

Miss Sally Ann Prindle was quite the little vixen. Sleek
as an otter and graceful as a cat. She had a peaches-and-

cream complexion, hair as shiny as a raven's wing and huge, innocent, luminous brown eyes. At the moment she was sitting on what might have been her finest feature, round and small and shapely. Longarm could not tell much about her tits as they were fashionably crushed to fit beneath the bodice of her traveling gown. Longarm, Jones, Bowman and the two other gents in the coach were all entranced by the maiden from Baltimore.

"That shooting in Evanston, miss, was no duel," Jones blurted. "It was an attempt on my very own life, that is what it was."

Sally Ann Prindle's eyes went wide. She gasped, and one delicately gloved hand went to her throat. And a very slender and pretty throat it was. "Are you the gentleman who . . ."

"Oh, no." Jones held up his wrist, which had handcuffs—and Ed Bowman—attached. "I am an important government witness, you see, in protective custody regarding a criminal case of great importance. This man"—he rather reluctantly inclined his head in Longarm's direction—"is guarding me. He is the one who did the actual, uh, shooting this morning. After the deceased attempted to assassinate me. It was a terrifying experience, believe me."

"Oh, I do, sir, I most assuredly do. And what are your names if you don't mind me asking. All of you?"

Each man introduced himself. In addition to Longarm and his charges there was Philip Dattely from Omaha and a skinny little fellow called Fats from Texas.

"Why, Mr. Fats, forgive me for my impertinence, please, but I was given to understand that all of you gentlemen from Texas were tall and handsomely formed. Like Mr. Long here."

"Texas men is big, miss," Fats drawled. The man seemed

somewhat the worse for wear, either still a little tipsy from last night or else getting a good start on it for the coming evening. "It's jus' that we ain't necessarily big in the parts that you can see."

Longarm damn near swallowed his tongue, but fortunately the brag appeared to go right over Sally Ann's pretty head.

The girl went chattering on, engaging one man after another in idle conversation. She was adorable if a trifle naïve. Longarm guessed her age at twenty or thereabouts but she was as innocent as a young girl. Cute. Definitely cute.

He pulled his eyes away from Miss Prindle to pay attention to the world that was passing outside the coach. Not that there was much to see, although the country here was positively lush in comparison with the barren land around Salt Springs, Nevada, where Ed Bowman had been hiding. Or even the high desert back at Fannin and Grady where Tomlin Jones was.

Since Longarm and the others had been the last ones to leave the train, they were put on the last coach as well. The last and the least desirable. Longarm was not even sure the rickety little son of a bitch deserved to be dignified with the term *coach*. He suspected it once might have been an army ambulance. But that was a generation or so back. Since then, the bodywork had eroded until now there was only a skeleton of an enclosure. Four seats, a floor and a roof held up by half a dozen—no, eight; he counted—upright posts. There was a luggage boot of sorts hanging off the back, but the usual roof rack was missing. The whole shebang probably would have collapsed if anyone put any more weight on those flimsy uprights. The driver sat on a slightly elevated seat up front. The rig was pulled by four bony and sweat-encrusted old horses.

The good news was that they would only be on the contraption long enough to get around to the other side of the break and return to the rails.

And Longarm was able to take some comfort in the knowledge that, slow as this wagon was moving, they were far enough behind the other coaches that their dust had time to settle before this outfit drove through it. So perhaps this tortuously slow little rig was not as uncomfortable as it might have been. At least the passengers were not breathing dirt like the folks would be in all but the leading coach up ahead.

Longarm's hand strayed toward his coat pocket where his cheroots were stored. Then, scowling, he took his hand away again. It would be an impertinence to light up in the presence of Miss Sally Ann Prindle. Damn it.

He could wait though. Had to, of course. But it should not be so terribly long. If he remembered correctly from the outward trip they would reach the rest station in another hour or two, then turn south again to get back to the tracks.

Even at this pace, he judged, they should return to the comforts of a Union Pacific passenger coach well before tomorrow's dawn.

At least that was the plan.

Longarm found his hand sliding inside his coat again without consciously willing it to and, annoyed with himself, he yanked it back and tried to think of something—anything—other than how good a smoke would taste just then. A smoke. Or a jolt from the bottle of rye he kept in his carpetbag. Or both. He would be damn-all glad to get to that rest station.

# Chapter 24

Shortly after dark Longarm heard a sharp crack and knew what had happened even before he felt the coach lurch suddenly to the right. *Down* and to the right. A wheel had broken.

"Damn," Longarm exclaimed, unmindful at that moment of Sally Ann on the seat opposite his. Bowman and Jones were seated side by side on the front seat where Longarm could keep an eye on them. Fats sat by himself on the rearmost bench. And Philip Dattely had managed to commandeer the most coveted position sitting next to Sally Ann.

Sally Ann yelped and held tight to her hat but she needn't have bothered. The coach was not going anywhere for a while.

"Shit!" the driver barked. Under other circumstances Longarm might have spoken to the man about his choice of language in the presence of a lady, but, as it was, Longarm could not blame him. "Whoa. Whoa, dammit."

The coach came to a halt, sagging perceptibly at the right front, and Longarm stepped down to the ground.

"Stay put, Miss Prindle. You other fellas come on down here. We'll help get that wheel changed an' be on our way in no time."

"Us, too?" Jones raised his hand, the one that had Ed Bowman hanging off his wrist.

"Yes, you, too, Mr. Jones."

Fats hopped over the side and dropped to the ground rather than bother waiting for the steps to clear. Bowman and Jones came down rather more gingerly. Dattely sat where he was, apparently unwilling to give up his position so close at Sally Ann's side.

The driver crawled off his box, grumbling and mumbling under his breath.

"Do you have a lantern?" Longarm asked.

"Nope. No damn lantern."

"It isn't going to be easy changing that wheel in the dark." There was some cloud overhead and the moon had not yet risen.

"Gonna be harder'n you think, mister. I ain't got no damn spare."

"You don't have . . ."

"Did when I started, mind you, but I onliest had the one an' I used it a'ready. The left side busted on my way down there this mornin'. Don't have no other."

Longarm opened his mouth to upbraid the fellow for not securing a replacement back there at the railroad. But that was not fair, he quickly realized. There was nothing at the tracks except a convenient place to stop and unload for the detour. No town, no camp, no services. Any repair or replacement would have to wait until the driver got his rig back home or . . . some damn place other than the middle of absolute nothing.

"Well, let's see how bad it is," Longarm said, hunkering down beside the broken wheel and running his hands over it.

What he found was not encouraging. At least one of the wooden spokes must have been broken for some time, allowing its load to be placed on the adjacent spokes. Now, three of the spokes were shattered and a fourth was badly cracked. The wheel, steel rim and all, had buckled and bent into a lopsided shape that resembled a figure-eight more than it did a proper circle. They would not be driving anywhere on this wheel.

"What about the wheel that broke before?" he asked. "Can you still use it enough to limp in on?"

"'Fraid not," the driver said. He turned his head and spat a stream of tobacco juice. "It's busted complete. 'Bout as bad as this 'un."

The jehu's chew reminded Longarm that not all the news was bad. Now that he was out of the coach he could have that smoke he'd been wanting. He fetched out a cheroot, nipped off the twist with his teeth and spat the bit of pale tobacco into the darkness before he struck a match and savored the pleasure of the smoke.

In the flare of Longarm's match, all of them could see just how badly broken the wheel was. It was even worse than Longarm had thought.

"What can we do?" Jones asked.

Longarm looked at the driver. "It's a good question, mister. What the devil *can* we do?"

"Wait."

"For what?"

"There'll be a string o' other coaches coming around this way with the westbound folks. We'll tell one o' them. Reckon they can send a wagon back for us or . . . somethin'. I ain't really sure." He sighed loudly. "Sure hope I get paid for this trip."

"Your pay is the least of our worries at the moment," Longarm told him.

"Not t' me it ain't," the driver returned.

"Will we be delayed long?" Sally Ann asked. "Why are you gentlemen not doing anything to fix the wheel? Does it really take all that long to do?"

Longarm explained the situation to her and, surprisingly, the girl chortled quite happily. "It is an adventure," she declared. "Stranded in the wilderness with all you handsome gentlemen. Oh, just wait until I tell my friends all about it. They shall be positively green with envy."

It was one point of view. Although not necessarily one that Longarm shared.

"You," the driver said, tugging Fats by the sleeve. "Come he'p me take these horses outta harness an' hobble them. They might as well see if can they find some graze while we's waiting."

Longarm stayed downwind of the wagon so the smoke from his cheroot would not bother the young lady.

There was nothing to do, he figured, but wait, just like the coach driver said. Someone was sure to be along by-and-by.

# Chapter 25

Along about two, three o'clock in the morning it became apparent that no westbound wagons were coming. By now any returning wagons should have passed. If there had been returning wagons.

The jehu dug a grimy fingernail into his whiskers, scratched vigorously in there and shook his head. "They must'a got the sumbish fixed an' the trains runnin' again. Said they might. Reckon they did."

"Do you mean we could just as easily have waited at the rail line for the repair work to be completed?" Dattely asked, his voice and demeanor indignant.

The driver only shrugged. But then he would not have been anxious for the passengers to wait while the last touches were put on the bridge repair. After all, he was paid by the trip. One more trip at the railroad's expense put that much more money in his pocket. He would have been happy to load his passengers at the last moment and skedaddle before the railroad superintendent changed his mind about sending the passengers around by coach.

"I reckon . . . ," the driver began. Then shook his head again. "I reckon I don't know what the hell t' do now. Wait, I s'pose."

"Wait for what?"

The man glanced toward the sky. Then toward the ground. Then to the east. Then the west. "I dunno. Just wait. Sumthin' oughta happen, we wait long enough."

Sally Ann squealed. And not with eager excitement this time. Longarm got the impression she no longer regarded this as some sort of wonderful adventure she could tell her chums over tea when she returned East.

"We will wait," Longarm said, "but only until morning. That homestead where we stopped on the outbound trip can't be too awfully far. Come daybreak we can rig some packs and load our luggage onto the horses and walk as far as the way station. They should have a wagon there or possibly some spare wheels. Anyway they'll be able to feed us. Prob'ly be happy to get some more customers at the railroad's expense. Does anybody have a better idea?"

No one did.

"All right then. Miss Prindle, you can sleep inside the coach. It's already chilly and there might be dew tonight. Be better if you stay inside for what little protection the roof will give. The menfolk can sleep on the ground underneath the coach or beside it."

"What about these handcuffs?" Jones asked. "I can't spend the night in chains."

"Oh, I'm betting that you can, Mr. Jones. You bein' such a fine runner . . . and me not bein' inclined to chase after you . . . I think you an' Mr. Bowman can keep each other company a little while longer."

Phil Dattely did not look particularly happy with the arrangement, but he had no better suggestion to offer. He grudgingly pulled his carpetbag out of the luggage boot and set it down beside one of the intact wheels where he could use it as a pillow, then crawled under the wagon and lay down.

Fats and the driver chose positions near the front of the rig, and a bitterly complaining Tomlin Jones hauled Edgar Bowman down to hands and knees so the two of them could crawl underneath.

Longarm helped Sally Ann inside, then turned away.

"Where will you sleep, Mr. Long?"

"Oh, I'll step off a little ways t' where it ain't so crowded, miss." He smiled. "I snore something awful, or so they tell me, and I wouldn't wanta keep everybody awake."

That part was a lie. The truth was that Longarm simply preferred his own company to that of strangers and, by habit, was wary of sleeping among them. His intention was to sit up and keep watch through the night. The loss of a little sleep would not hurt him. There were other things that might.

He touched the brim of his Stetson. "G'night, miss."

"Good night, Mr. Long."

By the time Longarm ambled off into the sand and sage, someone at the front of the coach, either Fats or the driver, was already snoring.

# Chapter 26

Half an hour or so later, the side of the rickety old coach tilted downward and the leather springs creaked softly in the night. The waist-high door swung open and a figure emerged, ghostly pale in the faint light from the stars overhead.

Sally Ann tiptoed quietly away from the sleeping men and out away from the rig. She headed more or less in Longarm's direction, walking more normally as she got farther away from the coach.

Probably had to pee, Longarm figured, and did not realize there was anyone awake to see. He would have remained completely silent so as to avoid embarrassing the girl but she stopped less than ten paces from where he was sitting and lifted the hem of her dress.

Longarm cleared his throat and faked a little cough, then said, "Good evenin', miss."

"Oh! There you are."

"What?"

"I was not sure just where you were, you see. And it is

very difficult to see you even knowing where you are. I could mistake you for a bush or a rock if you hadn't spoken."

"At night anything that's setting still will be like that. It's movement that draws the eye, you see. Wild animals know that. And Indians."

"How fascinating," Sally Ann said. He was not sure if the city girl was making fun of him or not. She continued to stand where she was, with the hem of her dress in both hands and the fabric lifted high enough that he could plainly see her legs from the knee down. Either she was wearing white stockings or she had removed her stockings for the night.

"D'you want me to, uh, go somewheres else?" he offered, still thinking she was looking for a spot where she could have some privacy.

"And make me follow you in this awful desert? I think not." She pulled the dress up higher and dragged it over her head, standing there in the night now wearing only her corset. Longarm could not help but notice that she did not seem to have any pantaloons on.

The girl came closer and stood before him, posing, turning, presenting herself for his inspection.

"Do you like?" she asked.

Yeah. He liked. She had plump little tits that peeked out from the top of her corset like a pair of fruits laid on a shelf, only the underslopes covered by the cloth while the rest of them all the way down to the small, dark nipples was on display.

Her waist was tiny, and he suspected that was no fault of the corset's tight strings.

Her hips swelled nicely below that waist, and her legs were slender. Between them lay a patch of dense fur, dark in the dim light of the night.

Her hair was quite tidily contained, suitable for an appearance in the most proper surroundings.

"Well?"

"Yes."

"Yes what?"

"Yes, I like what I see."

"You could tell a girl so."

It was late. He was sleepy—although he was plenty wide awake right now—and he was not exactly in the mood for games. "I just said so. Now what is it that you want? Other than getting naked where strangers can see, I mean?"

"Not strangers," she corrected. "Just one. Just you. Those others"—she gestured behind her—"they are all sleeping. I thought you would be asleep, too." She giggled. "I was going to surprise you."

"Congratulations," he said dryly. "You surprised me."

"You western men. You're so droll. But *so* handsome. And lean. I like a man who is lean and muscular. The boys back home . . . men, I suppose I should say, although they hardly seem like it . . . they are all so soft." She dropped the dress and came close. Reached up and laid a hand on Longarm's bicep. "You are anything but soft. You are strong. And . . . your gun. There is something about a man with a gun. . . ." She reached for his Colt.

"No," he said, capturing her wrist and gently but damn well insistently pulling her hand away.

"But I just . . ."

"No," he said again. "Guns aren't for playing with."

"They are very exciting, you know."

"A gun is a tool, lady. Just another tool."

"You can say that, but I doubt you believe it." She shrugged and smiled. "Not that it matters anyway. I didn't come out here to talk about guns."

"Look, I don't mean to sound ungrateful or anything. You're real pretty. An' I mean that. But just what the hell did you walk out here for, Miss Prindle?"

She cocked her pretty little head to one side and laughed softly. "La, sir. I came out here to see if you would do me the favor of a good, hearty fuck."

Longarm threw his head back and laughed. He had to stifle the sound of it or he would have awakened everyone at the wagon and any creatures within a half mile around.

"Well?" she demanded.

"I think we can manage something along those lines, miss."

"Under the circumstances, sir, you might consider calling me Sally Ann."

Longarm did not say anything in response to that.

He merely reached out for her and pulled her in close against him.

# Chapter 27

Her breath was hot, her kisses frantic. She wrapped herself around him so tightly he thought she was trying to come inside and become a part of his body. Her tongue invaded his mouth, and Sally Ann shuddered when he touched her breast. He was not sure but he thought she might actually have reached a climax just from that. The girl had a hair trigger. Which was perfectly fine by him.

He reached down for his belt buckle and Sally Ann pulled away long enough to gulp in a quick breath then say, "No. Leave it on. Leave everything on. Let me take care of it. Please."

Ever the gent, Longarm did not argue with the lady. He took his hand away and let her take care of it.

Sally Ann reattached herself to his face, sucking on his tongue like she intended to pull it out if she could. Her hands, however, were busy elsewhere. She left his belt and gunbelt alone, instead unfastening only the buttons at his fly.

She reached inside his britches and found the opening at the front of his drawers, reached inside there and gasped when she felt the magnitude of Longarm's pecker.

"Oh, my. Now you've surprised me, sir." She laughed. "That is a weapon even more interesting than your gun. May I play with this one, please?"

"Mmm, I think that'd be all right."

She wrapped her fingers tight around it and sighed, then pulled it out of his trousers.

"Lovely," she murmured. "Simply lovely."

She dropped to the ground, tugging on his hand to urge him down with her, and stretched out on the hard, gravel-littered desert surface.

She had to be lying on stones and twigs and perhaps even the tiny button cactuses that grew in such profusion here, but she was insistent that he lie on top of her.

Longarm offered no argument. He moved between her wide open legs and lowered himself onto her as gently as possible.

"No. Hard. I like it rough. Take me now. Please."

The Colt was pressing into her belly. He knew good and well it was because he could feel the holster pushing hard into the left side of his belly. Yet when he tried to remove it so as to make her more comfortable she stopped him.

"Please. Please," she whispered hoarsely. "Just . . . take me. Fill me. Please."

Longarm pulled his hips back just enough to let his cock slide down the soft fur of her pubic hair and into the hot, wet socket that lay hidden within.

"Oh! Yes," Sally Ann cried out when he pressed himself into her.

The girl's body was trembling.

"All. All of it. Yesssssss!"

130

Longarm plunged into her. Dug his toes into the ground for leverage and rammed it home. Pulled back and slammed into her again. Harder. Harder. Faster.

Sally Ann whimpered and gasped. Her hands clutched convulsively, and she would have clawed his back to ribbons if he hadn't still had his coat on.

She wrapped her legs around Longarm's waist, lifting her hips to give him better access and urging him on.

"Harder. Oh, yes. Harder."

Hell, Longarm was already afraid he was going to break her in two.

But if she wanted it harder. . . .

He jammed himself into her small body like he was trying to drive all the way through and out the other side. He slammed his hard, male body onto her soft, receptive one, and Sally Ann kept up with him, meeting his every thrust with a matching one of her own.

He felt the tremors of her climaxes once, twice . . . he lost track after the first five or six, and the harder he pounded her the better she liked it and the more she came.

His own bursting rush of satisfaction came all too quickly. For both of them.

He grunted with one final effort to batter her and stiffened while his juices spewed hot and sticky deep inside her.

Sally Ann cried out as she came again as well.

"Shh," he warned. "They'll hear."

"I don't care," she gasped. "I just hate that it's over so soon."

Longarm grinned. "Over, hell. All that done is t' take the edge off. Let me stroke nice an' slow for a few seconds to build a head o' steam an' we'll go at it again."

"You can't be serious." But she sounded very much like she hoped that, indeed, he was serious.

"Hey, if you don't want any more. . . ." He moved as if to pull out.

"No," she said frantically. "Don't . . . don't do that. I want more. I want everything. You can really do it again? Honest?"

"Of course. Say, aren't you lying on stones and stuff. D'you want me to find a blanket or something?"

"No. Don't go. I'm fine."

"Isn't your butt sore?"

"As a boil," she said happily. "I shall feel this for the next week." She laughed. "If I'm lucky. Now . . . oh! I can feel something else right now. You're ready again, aren't you? You really are!"

"Tell you what," Longarm said. "Let's see can we scrub your pretty little ass onto the rocks bad enough so's you feel it for a second week, too."

"Yes." She giggled. "Please."

Longarm did his level best to accommodate the lady.

# Chapter 28

Longarm lay dozing in that delightful twilight state of less than full wakefulness yet he was not really asleep either. He felt good despite being worn down to a nubbin by the night's exertions. Drained? Lordy, he felt like he'd been pumped out.

Which, considering how vigorously the little lady could suck a cock, he kind of had. She was good. Almighty good.

At the moment, she lay sleeping at his side. He would have to wake her in a moment because it was coming dawn, the sky already beginning to pale, and she would have to return to the wagon before any of the others woke up and discovered where she'd spent the night. He certainly did not want to ruin her reputation.

It was a funny thing, Longarm mused. A man could do pretty much what he pleased and no one would fault him so long as he remained reasonably respectful of life, law and property.

But a woman? One hint of mischief, even innocent fun that was outside the boundaries of normal, and she might as well be branded to show she was a tramp. Just lay the iron to both cheeks and her forehead and be done with it.

It was not fair. Longarm understood that. He was pretty sure everyone else realized it, too. But it was the way things were and there was no way to get around that.

He was thinking about silliness like that when he felt the girl stir and ever so stealthily shift away from him.

Through half-closed eyes he watched as she came onto all fours and then stood up. He was so thoroughly sated that even the sight of her fluffing out her hair—it had come adrift at some point during their play—wearing nothing but a corset failed to get a rise out of him.

That was all right. There wasn't time enough to jump her again anyway.

Sally Ann bent and picked up the dress she'd shucked to start it all. In the near dark, she seemed to be having trouble figuring out what was the front and what was the back.

"Need some help?" he offered, sitting up and reaching into his coat pocket for a cigar. It was damned convenient this sleeping—and fucking—fully dressed. But even so, not something he figured to do on a regular basis.

Sally Ann gasped and dropped her dress.

"Sorry. I didn't mean t' startle you," Longarm said. He dipped two fingers into his vest pocket and pulled out a match, then bit the twist off the end of his cheroot and lighted the dark, slim cylinder. The smoke tasted good. Would have tasted even better if he'd had something to rinse the night fur out of his mouth first, but the canvas water bag was back at the wagon. He would take a quick piss and go have a swig out of the bag, then be ready for whatever the day might bring.

"You . . . you did, yes."

"Sorry," he repeated.

Sally Ann bent and retrieved the dress, then hurriedly sorted it out and pulled it on. "I have to get back before the others wake up."

"Uh, huh." Longarm stood, thinking to give the girl a kiss to send her on her way but by the time he came upright she had already turned and was hurrying back to the disabled coach.

Sally Ann had been a regular lovebird the whole night long. Now she practically acted like she was afraid of him.

Oh, well. The day a man started trying to understand a woman was the day he might as well go check himself into the lunatic asylum that Ed Bowman escaped from—for no man born has ever fully understood the least complex of women.

And a wild and horny little thing like Sally Ann Prindle who liked pain along with her fucking? No, sir. It was a fool's game to try and second guess one like that.

Longarm stuck his cigar into the corner of his mouth and turned to find a likely spot to piss on. Because, after all, a fellow doesn't want to let fly at just any old rock or weed. You want to feel right about where you make water.

# Chapter 29

It was a three-hour walk to the way station, and, by the time they, arrived Longarm was heartily sick of listening to Tomlin Jones bitch and moan. Who the hell would have thought that it would be the runner who hated walking so damn much?

And, on top of that, his feet hurt. And he was near out of cigars. And he hadn't gotten a wink of sleep the whole night. And he was hungry. And . . . and he just wasn't in a very good humor, now that was the fact of the matter.

Thank goodness they had the horses to take care of the luggage and to carry Sally Ann or it would have been even worse. Longarm tried to find consolation in that fact. Tried to, but it didn't make his feet hurt less or Jones's complaints any easier to take.

"Thank goodness," Fats mumbled as they finally reached the handful of buildings beside a narrow creek where the farmer and his family were trying to scratch out a living.

"Ah, breakfast," Bowman said quite cheerfully. Of them

all, Longarm would say Edgar Bowman the lunatic complained the least. But then there was no telling what sort of treatment he had been accustomed to receiving at the asylum back in Utah.

Come to think of it, Longarm couldn't for the life of him figure out what it was about Ed Bowman that was supposed to be crazy. Not that Custis Long knew anything about the subject. He supposed the doctors did. It seemed odd, that was all.

"I want a steak," Jones announced. "I want it this thick." He demonstrated with his thumb and middle finger to suggest a piece of meat that would surely be a roast not a steak. "And I want eggs. Three of them fried in bacon grease. And fried potatoes. And . . ."

"Shut up, Jones. You'll eat the same as the rest of us."

Longarm reached up to help Sally Ann down from the bony back of a ratty-looking brown horse. "You look uncomfortable," he said in a low tone. "Hurting a little, are you?"

"Terrible," she said. She did not sound as if she were at all unhappy with the fact. Quite the contrary, actually.

Longarm set her lightly on her feet and turned the horse over to the jehu, whose name was Vance something—or possibly it was something Vance, Longarm was not sure—and escorted Sally Ann inside.

"We wasn't expecting anybody else," the farmer said. "You folks part of that railroad detour?"

"Yes, dagnabbit," Dattely explained. "Our wagon broke down. We're tired and we're hungry and we need to get back to the railroad."

The farmer stuffed a finger into his nose and swirled it around in there for a moment before he spoke. "You think the railroad will pay us like they said they'd do?"

"If they agreed to it before, they will still stand behind it," Longarm assured the man.

"You are of that?"

"I'm sure," Longarm told him although the promise was conjectural in nature.

"All right then." The farmer turned to his wife, who was about half his age and whose belly was swollen with child. "Cook for 'em. The usual."

"I want a steak," Jones began. "About this thick, and . . ."

"You'll eat what I eat, mister," the farmer snapped. "If you don't want what my old lady fixes, then don't eat. That's all right by me. But hush up. If you wanta grumble, you can do it outside 'cause you're not gonna come into my home under my roof and be telling me what-for. Understand that, do you?"

Jones turned to Longarm. "I want . . ."

"The gentleman told you, Jones. Shut up."

"The U.S. attorney is going to hear about this."

"Fine. You tell him. When we get back t' Denver I'll get you the paper and ink so's you can write him a complete report on how you been treated. In the meantime, though, shut up."

By then the farmer's wife had already escorted Sally Ann to a seat at the table. The woman, who was probably even younger than Sally Ann but who spoke with the authority of impending motherhood, clucked and fussed over her young visitor.

Ed Bowman headed for a place at the table, dragging Jones along with him at the end of the chain that joined them, and Phil Dattely took a seat next to Sally Ann. Longarm chose a place deliberately far from Sally Ann, leaving room for Vance and Fats, who came in before the plain meal was ready: rice and red beans with vinegar and salt to pour on.

"Coffee will be ready in a minute," the farmer's wife said. She sounded apologetic.

"This is fine, ma'am," Longarm assured her, shoving a heaping spoonful of the mixture past his mustache. "Real good in fact. We're beholden to you."

The pregnant girl blushed, and Longarm got the impression she did not get much in the way of compliments.

"If you'all don't mind riding in the back of a farm wagon instead of on the seats of a fine coach, I can carry you down to the railroad," the farmer said. "Be quicker and easier than trying to fix the wheels on your own rig. Then Vance and me can come back and finish taking care of his coach."

"Sounds fine," Longarm said.

"Excellent," Dattely agreed.

"Finish up then. We can leave as soon as everyone's had a chance to, uh, use the facility and wash up."

# Chapter 30

It was well past noon by the time they finished hitching Vance's team to the farmer's wagon.

"Apt to be dark before we get down there," the farmer said. "You'all could stay the night if you like."

"I think we should," Sally Ann quickly said. "Riding in the dark frightens me."

Longarm was pretty sure that was a lie. Despite her innocent appearance Longarm doubted she was afraid of much of anything. He figured she just wanted one more night of down and dirty fucking before she had to submit herself to the rules of polite society again. And while there is not a thing in the world wrong with a night spent humping a good-looking little old gal, he did have obligations to meet.

For his part of it, the farmer probably wanted to assure himself of being paid by the railroad for that much more room and board. The man's hardscrabble farm was hardly a prosperous proposition out here, and the railroad's payment might be the only cash money he could count on seeing this year.

"We'll go on," Longarm quickly said.

"What makes you think you can decide," the farmer challenged.

"Official United States government business," Longarm said, pulling out his wallet to display his badge. "We'll go on. Now."

The farmer obviously did not like it, but he accepted the decision without argument. He and Vance and Fats went about loading the luggage.

Sally Ann looked nervous for some reason. Jumpy. Longarm couldn't figure out why that should be so. She had been well and truly banged just a matter of hours earlier and was still sore and hurting from that experience. So disappointed? Sure. But not jumpy.

But there he went again trying to figure out a woman. That is always a stupid thing for a man to do. Hell, it's probably a stupid thing for another woman to do, too, strange as they all seem to be.

"I need to go take a shit," Jones announced.

"Don't be using language like that around the lady again," Longarm warned. "I won't have it."

"I will do anything I please," Tomlin Jones retorted.

"Fine, an' so will I. That could include trussing you up like a hog ready for the spit and shoving a dirty sock in your mouth to keep you quiet if I take the notion."

"You wouldn't."

"Try me," Longarm growled.

"Come on, man. Let's go," Bowman said, once again tugging at their chain to pull Jones along behind.

Longarm scowled as he watched them disappear around to the back of the farmhouse.

When he turned back again Sally Ann had disappeared. Probably went inside to say good-bye to the pregnant girl, Longarm figured.

Fats and Vance followed the farmer indoors while Philip Dattely climbed into the wagon to assure himself of a comfortable spot.

Longarm figured he ought to take another leak while he had the chance. The outhouse was full. He knew that. Fortunately he was not in need of the shitter, just a place where he could get out of sight from the womenfolk.

He ambled along toward the farmer's ramshackle little harness shed, thinking to step around behind it.

When he did he came to a sudden halt.

He'd found Sally Ann Prindle.

She was standing at the back of the shed, leaning against the corner facing the outhouse.

That would have been well and good except for one small thing.

The girl held her wrist steadied against the wall and she had a nickel-plated pocket pistol in her hand. The little gun was cocked and aimed toward the outhouse door where in another minute or so Tomlin Jones and Edgar Bowman would emerge.

No wonder she'd seemed nervous. She was about to commit an assassination.

Why the hell would . . .

Longarm heard the door spring creak as the shitter door was pushed open.

Sally Ann bent to peer over the sights of her pistol. Longarm could see her finger commence to tighten on the trigger.

"Stop!" he roared, just as loud and angry as he could.

The idea was that she should be distracted. Panic. Hell, maybe even drop the revolver.

The pretty little thing was made of sterner stuff than he'd realized.

At the sound of Longarm's voice she did not hesitate. She spun around to face him and dropped into a crouch, the muzzle of her pistol lining up on Longarm's belly.

Once again the girl's finger began to close on the trigger.

# Chapter 31

The sound of Longarm's shout had not really unnerved the girl, but the sight of his big Colt pointing at her certainly did.

She rushed her shot, the little Ivor Johnson .38 barking like an angry lapdog, but its bullet sailed just wide of his ribs.

Longarm, on the other hand, fired with deliberate speed. The double-action Colt roared and Sally Ann staggered backward, then sank to her knees.

Longarm was kneeling at her side before she had time to lie flat on the hard, stony ground. His first order of business was to pluck the revolver out of her fingers and stuff it into his coat pocket. Sally Ann seemed to have resigned from the assassination business, her interests suddenly lying elsewhere, but a man who wants to keep on living knows better than to take chances.

He tenderly laid her down, cradling her on his arm with her head in the crook of his elbow.

Sally Ann looked at him, her eyes wide with disbelief. A

tear welled up in the corner of one eye and rolled down her cheek into her ear.

"Maybe this isn't so bad," he said although he knew damned good and well that it was. His slug had taken her in the right side of the chest, squarely over the soft tit that, just hours before, he had licked and suckled and enjoyed so very much.

At the very least, Sally Ann's lung was punctured, but that would be the least of her worries. A large caliber bullet impacting there could have shattered a rib and sent sharp splinters of bone throughout the soft internal tissues.

A pale red froth appeared on the girl's lips and grew into a bubble. Sunlight reflected in the shiny surface of the bubble and created a tiny rainbow there. The bubble disappeared when Sally Ann moved her lips to speak.

"I never . . . meant."

"Hush now. It's all right, girl."

"What happened?" a man's voice asked. Longarm glanced up to see Jones and Bowman standing there. The others, the farmer and the jehu and the other passengers, were hurrying to join them. Longarm ignored them.

"Hurts, Long. It hurts. Not . . . a good hurt . . . this time. But last night . . . won . . . derful. That was . . . wonderful . . . thank you."

He smiled at her and smoothed a wisp of sweat-soaked hair back from her forehead.

"You're gonna be fine," he lied. She was slipping away. God knew what sort of damage was inside her, but he had no doubt that she was dying.

"Never meant . . . you . . . shoot you . . . never meant to . . ."

"I know, girl. I know you didn't." He bent down and

lightly kissed her, the taste of her blood on his lips when he did so. "It's all right, Sally Ann."

"No. Not . . . Sal . . . name is . . . is Emma . . . Lucille . . . Swain. Put that on marker . . . please."

"Emma Lucille Swain. Got it."

"He said . . . five hundred dollars . . . done a lot of . . . crazy things. Never saw . . . that much money before. Ever. Five hun'erd. Lot of . . . money."

"He?" Longarm asked. "Who hired you, Emma? Who hired you to shoot Jones?"

"Jo . . . Jo . . . ?" He was losing her. He could feel the life force draining out of the girl's body as surely as he could see the fluttering rise and fall of her bullet-shattered chest.

Her eyes went wide and she looked furiously back and forth but seemed not to see.

Her lips parted and in a clear, strong voice she asked, "What?" as if she were responding to a question no one on this Earth could hear.

And then she was gone. Her slim body sagged and seemed to deflate, becoming even smaller in death.

"What the hell happened here?"

"Why'd you shoot Miss Prindle, Long? Are you mad?"

"Oh Jesus, I'm gonna throw up."

Longarm paid no attention to any of them. He stood, picking Sally Ann—no, dammit, Emma—picking Emma up when he did so, and carried her into the shade of the farmer's shed.

They would wrap her body and bury her here in the hard soil of a harsh land. She might have liked that, he thought. And, at the next town they came to, he would pay for a marker to be carved and sent back to put on the grave. Emma Lucille Swain it would read. No more, for he did not even know what dates to give to the man who formed it. Just the name.

Five hundred dollars though. It was a hell of a lot of money for one shot. Even so, he wondered if she really thought she could get away with murder when he was so close by. She must surely have had something in mind, although she could not claim an attempted rape. Not unless she shot both Jones and Ed Bowman, too, lest he act as a witness against her. Or possibly last night's play had been an attempt to blunt Longarm's fangs so he would be madly enamored of her. Enough to let her get away with murder? No damn way. But she might not have known that, might have thought it worth a try.

One thing was for sure. Longarm would never know now what the girl had had in mind, not last night and not just now either.

He placed her limp body down on the frame of the farmer's hay rake.

He had had better days than this one was proving to be.

# Chapter 32

Joe. Was that what she'd been trying to say in those last moments of the girl's life? Was it somebody named Joe who hired her? Joe *who*, dammit? Who was he? Where was he? When did he hired her? Damn.

Longarm let the farmer's wife take over what needed to be done for Emma, the washing and the combing and the laying out. He dragged her bag out of the wagon and jimmied the ineffective brass lock. There were two dresses inside, one of them quite nice, and some underthings.

He shook out the nicer of the dresses and handed it to Bowman. "You two take this dress to the lady so's she can put it on Miss Swain."

"Who is Miss Swain?"

"Sally Ann. Swain is her real name. Emma Swain. The dress she's been traveling in is bloodstained. I don't want her buried in it. She should be dressed nice. And tell the farmer I'll be sending a headstone back from Cheyenne to mark the grave. When you're done with that, gather the others an' get them back here. We got to be going. There's nothing left here t' be done or said."

The trip down to the railroad was spent mostly in silence. None of the other men seemed to know what to think of Longarm now. Or what to say.

Hell, he wasn't pleased about any of it either. But he hadn't had any choice in the matter. Sally Ann—Emma—was intent on murder back there. He had to stop her. Had to keep her from shooting him, too. He had not had any damn choice. None.

But he hated it anyway.

When they finally reached the tracks sometime in the night, there was no one there. They could see where the temporary camp had been for the railroad work crew and for the passenger accommodation. All of that was abandoned now, leaving only flattened grass, bare fire rings and piles of horse shit where the livestock had been tethered while awaiting the arrival of the next batch of passengers to be driven around the break in the rails.

"What are we going to do now?"

"Wait. Stop the next train coming east," Longarm said.

"How do you propose to do that?"

Longarm's smile held no warmth in it. "Oh, they'll stop. We are gonna plant a bonfire square on those tracks over there. A big one. They see that, they'll stop."

"I don't know that's such a good idea," Vance said.

"Are you thinking of an extra fee for taking us on t' the next town? Forget it. We are gonna continue on from here in comfort."

# Chapter 33

When they finally were able to board an eastward-bound Union Pacific train in the small hours of the night, Longarm found himself unable to sleep. He could normally just tip his hat over his eyes and drop off instantly, but this night proved to be long and miserable.

He'd had no choice about shooting the girl, dammit. Yet the killing haunted him anyway. She had been so young. So pretty. With so much to live and look forward to . . . if she'd only allowed it.

By the time they reached Cheyenne, in the late afternoon, he was exhausted. And he still had shopping to do before he could carry on to Denver and the end of this job.

"Look," he told his charges, "I'm worn out. I got to get some sleep. Got to find a stonemason, too, and I don't want to be spending all my time looking over my shoulder to see is anybody lyin' in wait with a gun. I'm gonna put the both of you in a proper cell here. They'll hold you overnight an' I'll see you're fed good and protected. Besides which it'll mean you get t' stretch out an' sleep without those handcuffs chafing your wrists any more."

"I don't want jail food, dammit. Take us to dinner before we go into a cell," Jones complained.

"I wasn't askin' your permission, mister. I was tellin' you what's gonna happen just so's you'd know." Longarm glared at Tomlin Jones, then turned his attention to Ed Bowman. "D'you got anything to say?"

"Not me. Whatever you say is fine with me."

"Well, all right, then. The county sheriff's office an' jail is just down this way. It has nicer cells than the city jail an' it ain't so likely you'll be bothered by loud drunks in the county lockup. Now, let's go."

Longarm had spent considerable time in Cheyenne over the years and was already acquainted with Charlie Logan, the deputy who was on duty that afternoon.

"No problem, Longarm. We'll be glad to look after your prisoners," Charlie told him. "Are they violent? Anything special we should look out for?"

"Naw, they're all right. Don't let any visitors in to see 'em, though. There's somebody gunning for the big one there. Don't want him to testify against his old boss, an' there might could be some folks around Cheyenne who wouldn't want him doing that. He don't need to visit with old friends anyway."

"Consider it done. No visitors for either of them. Understand that I won't be able to keep people from finding out they're here, though. There's always somebody coming and going back there. Prisoners and lawyers and visitors and such."

"That's all right. Just keep them off to themselves if you can. And feed them good, Charlie. The big one eats a lot. Gonna turn into a regular walrus if he sits in a cell for very long without working off all that grub he chokes down."

"I heard that, Long," Jones snapped. "I shall inform the United States attorney about the treatment I've received at your hands."

"You do that, Jones. An' when you do, remember t' be thankful that you're still alive to tell him all about it."

To the deputy Longarm said, "I'll check the train schedules in the morning, Charlie, an' be back to pick 'em up sometime in the forenoon."

"They'll be here whenever you get around to them, Longarm."

"Thanks, Charlie. You're a good man." Longarm smiled and added, "Never mind what the sheriff says about you when you ain't listening."

Logan laughed and took charge of Tomlin Jones and Edgar Bowman, leading the two of them away toward the modern steel cellblock provided by the good taxpayers of Laramie County, Wyoming Territory.

Longarm felt like a free man when he stepped outside unburdened of the responsibility for those two lives. Charlie Logan could see to them for the time being, and that was just fine.

He walked downtown to Rentzler's Chop House and treated himself to a good feed, then checked his pocket watch to make sure he would be in time to catch the stonemason before the close of normal business hours. He was. Barely.

Longarm had never done business with Newcomb's Stoneworks before but he had seen the place time and again when he was in Cheyenne. It would have been hard to miss. It was situated close by the railroad tracks and had a small loading dock out back, presumably so Newcomb could more easily ship his stone creations.

The front yard was a silent advertisement to the man's

153

expertise. It held dozens of headstones in marble and polished granite, already carved except for the names and dates to be added. Flanking a gate in the low fence surrounding the property were a pair of exquisitely carved angels done in white marble, each of them looking like the angel could spring into flight at any moment. Beside the door to the office and workshop was a handsomely wrought black marble statue depicting a bird dog on point with a downed duck in its mouth.

Longarm heard the jangle of a small bell when he pulled the gate open and, a moment later, a squat, broadly build man with a dark beard and small, friendly eyes appeared at the side.

"Are you Newcomb?"

"That's me. But you can call me Mr. Newcomb if you like." He was smiling when he said it.

"How's about *sir*. Would sir be good for you?" Longarm extended his hand. He liked this Newcomb fellow.

"Hmm. Sir Newcomb. Yes, I might could accept that. And you would be . . ."

"Long. Longarm to my friends. I hope you'll call me Longarm."

"In that case, you can call me Kerry. Or Newk. Most of my friends call me Newk, Longarm."

"Newk it shall be then, friend. I'm here t' pick out a stone. Something pretty as it's for a young lady. Maybe with some flowers and . . . hell, Newk, I don't know. Help me out here, will you?"

Newcomb took Longarm by the elbow and guided him into the forest of headstones. "Don't worry. We'll take care of it, you and me."

"Thanks. T' tell you the truth, I could . . . I could use the help."

It was almost dark by the time Longarm and Newcomb worked out the details of the stone and the style of lettering and delivery, but Longarm was satisfied. The girl he had known as Sally Ann Prindle would have a marker to make her proud, and the rest of it would soon enough be forgotten.

He was pleased, but very tired, by the time he walked back in town to the Drover's Rest hotel to check in. He was leaning on the desk, waiting for the clerk to emerge from the hotel office, when he heard a loud challenge behind his back.

"You!" a woman's voice shouted. "Long."

Oh, dear Lord. Another one. Longarm dropped into a crouch and spun around, his Colt already in hand.

# Chapter 34

The girl screamed when she saw the blue steel of the gun swinging to aim squarely at her. Her eyes rolled back in her head and she dropped into a dead faint, falling hard onto a Persian rug on the hotel lobby floor.

Longarm was so startled himself that he damn near pulled the trigger. He stopped himself barely in time to avoid applying the final few ounces of pressure that would have fired the big revolver.

He leaped forward, but was not in time to prevent the unconscious girl from landing on the floor. Only when he was kneeling beside her did he finally recognize the young actress he had last seen in Denver just before he left to head west. It took him several confused moments to recall her name. Esme. He did not remember her last name, but the first name was Esme. He was sure of that. Hell, he still had the list she had given him showing when and where her theatrical troupe would be performing. The list lay in his pocket, completely forgotten since the moment she gave it to him.

"Sir? Sir! Please explain yourself, sir." The desk clerk had finally put in an appearance and was not at all happy with Longarm about this disturbance in the lobby.

"Calm down. I'm a deputy U.S. marshal and a friend o' the young lady here."

"Then why did you . . ."

"Mister, shut the hell up. Just give me a washcloth and a basin o' cool water so's I can bring her around. Then point me toward her room." Longarm gave the man a stare that was cold and hard enough to put the shivers into his bones.

"Yes, sir," the clerk said, his belligerence wilting under the force of that look. He snapped his fingers impatiently at the bellboy who had come to try to help. "You heard the gentleman. Water. And a hand towel. Be quick about it."

"Yes, sir, Mr. Johnson," the bellboy squeaked before bolting off toward the back of the place. He was back within moments offering Longarm the requested implements.

Longarm dabbed a corner of the towel into the cold water, then gently bathed Esme's cheeks and forehead. After a few seconds she moaned and began to stir.

Her eyes popped wide in fright when she came fully awake again, but she relaxed when she saw Longarm bending over her.

"Sorry I gave you such a turn," he said softly.

The girl smiled. "I didn't expect . . . you know."

"It's a long story," he said.

"I have time to listen," she suggested. "We don't open until the matinee tomorrow. And I happen to be without plans for this evening."

"Then consider yourself t' have the evening all booked up. We'll have the best this ol' town can offer. Have fresh oysters and French champagne brought up t' your room. How would that be?"

Her smile became even bigger. "As long as you are with me, Custis, I'd be happy with hardtack and tepid water."

"You're sweet," he said. Then laughed. "But it's plain you never tried hardtack. D'you think you can walk? Or would you like for me t' carry you to your room?"

"Carry me." She seemed delighted by the prospect. "I would love for you to carry me in your arms."

"Then show me the way, little girl." He scooped her up off the floor and stood, took a moment to get his balance and said, "Where're we going?"

Esme giggled. "I'm on the fourth floor."

Longarm rolled his eyes but started dutifully up the stairs. Esme stopped him, though, and asked to be put down onto her feet at the top of the first flight of stairs. "I don't want to waste any of your strength," she said with an impish look in her eyes. "Let's save that for a much more rewarding sort of exercise, shall we?"

Longarm laughed and set her lightly onto her feet. "Lead the way, pretty girl."

Funny thing, but he no longer felt half as tired as he'd been just a few minutes earlier.

# Chapter 35

Longarm woke to find Esme's pretty face only a few inches from his own. She had her head propped on the palm of one hand and was smiling.

"What the . . . !"

Esme laughed. "Sleepyhead. Just when things were getting interesting you fell asleep on me. I mean that, too. Really and truly *on* me. You were lying on top of me . . . and inside me . . . and the next thing I knew you were snoring."

"I wasn't!"

"All right. Not snoring. Exactly. But you were certainly breathing awfully deep. You must have been exhausted."

"Reckon I was." He was starting to remember now. And yes, he'd been exhausted. And still thinking about Sally Ann Prindle. Lying there with Esme but thinking about the girl he'd killed. And then he just sort of . . . went away. "I was on top o' you?"

"Yes." She laughed again. "I liked it. The closeness. Then you started to feel heavy on me. You know? So I wiggled out from under you, real slow. Did it without waking you, though you stirred and mumbled a little. And you've been like that this whole night long." She gave him an impish smile, her nose wiggling just a little. "Custis, do you know something? You look kind of sweet when you're sleeping. I can see what you must have looked like when you were a little boy."

Smiling, she dragged a fingertip across his cheek. "That was before you got these whiskers, of course. I swear, you're like a bristle brush now. Like some old scrub brush."

"It's been a couple days since I've had a shave," he admitted.

"You don't say!"

"I, uh, take it you figured that out already," he said.

"Yes. But I don't mind. I even like that about you. And the way your body looks, so lean and hard and powerful. I let the lamp burn and stayed awake all night just looking at you. And smelling you. You have the most marvelous scent. Masculine. I can only think of one odor that is better and that is the scent of your come. I remember how good that smells." Her expression became serious. "Custis. May I please have your come?"

"I . . ."

"No, don't move. Please don't move. Just roll a little so that you're on your back and then lie still, will you? I want to do this. I don't want you to move, not a single muscle. Let me, Custis. Please."

She placed her hand on his chest and pressed him flat to the bed. Longarm offered no resistance.

Esme raised up on one elbow and bent over him. Her face—soft lips, huge eyes, delicate nose—filled his field of vision. She brought her face closer and began to nibble delicately at him using only her lips. Then the tip of her tongue.

She very lightly licked his eyelids and eyelashes. Ran her

tongue over his nose and into first one nostril and then the other. Longarm found that feeling strange but not unpleasant.

Her tongue explored inside his upper lip, then found its way inside his left ear. Down onto his throat. And lower, onto the hard planes of Longarm's chest.

"No," she murmured. "Don't move. Let me do this."

He had no damn idea of moving. Fact was, he was enjoying this. It seemed a helluva fine way to wake up.

He did moan a little, though, when Esme's talented tongue found his left nipple. She sucked gently while the tip of that pink little tongue titillated the tiny nubbin. The feel of it sent a tingling sensation all the way down into his groin. He could feel his balls begin to swell. His cock had long since come to rigid attention in response to the girl's ministrations.

"Ah!" he breathed.

"Shh. Hush, dear. Don't move."

It was damn-all difficult not to, but he tried to go limp and let himself do nothing but feel what Esme was doing.

She moved slowly across his chest to the other nipple, and that one proved to be even more sensitive and responsive than the first had been. Very much against his will, Longarm's hips began to pulse very slightly up and down as his cock sought the wet heat that would bring joyous release.

He jackknifed upright when Esme ran her tongue inside his navel, but she pushed him down flat again with a whispered, "Don't, dearest, don't."

Then her tongue was on the shaft of his cock and everything else was forgotten. She licked him thoroughly, moved down to his balls and cupped them in the warmth of her palm. Lifted them so she could lick and suckle each one, then moved up onto his shaft again.

Longarm groaned.

"I'm thirsty, dear. Give me your juice. Let me drink it down, every drop."

Her mouth enveloped him and her tongue swirled around and around the head, the tip of it managing to slide underneath the foreskin and drive him into a frenzy, thrusting upward to drive his cock deep into her mouth.

Esme pulled away. "Lie still, dear. Be still."

Longarm was not at all sure he could comply. But he lay back again and willed himself not to move again no matter what Esme did.

The girl smiled and kissed the head then rained butterfly kisses up and down his shaft for a moment before she once again took him into her mouth.

Longarm very nearly came there and then. She took him deep and applied suction, her cheeks hollow with effort as she attempted to pull the come out of him.

Finally, at long last she began to bob her head slowly up and down while continuing to suck. Slowly. Slowly. And then quicker. Quicker still.

She opened her mouth wide and thrust downward onto Longarm's pole, driving the full length of him beyond her mouth and deep into her throat.

He could feel the rings of cartilage in her throat parting at the intrusion. Could feel her lips wrap tight around the base of his cock and her chin hard on his groin.

"Ahhhhhhh!" Longarm cried out. He could not help himself. And he thrust upward with his hips in a sudden spasm as his come came gushing out to spurt in ecstatic release deep inside Esme's throat.

The girl patiently retained him in her mouth, still sucking, until he had no more seed to give her. Only then did she allow him to slide, wet and shiny, out into the steamy air.

"That tastes as good as it smells. Did you know that?"

He was almost too wiped out to speak but managed to say, "No, reckon I didn't at that."

"Take my word for it, dear. You taste marvelous good. But I wish I'd saved some of it to wipe on my face so I could smell your come through the day."

"Tell you what," Longarm said. "Give me a little while t' recover, an' I'll let you have s' more of that stuff. You can do whatever you like with this next bunch."

Esme laughed. "I shall take you up on that, dear. Now close your eyes and rest for just a little. And this next time I want to feel you inside me. Will you do that for me, Custis?"

"It's a promise," he said, closing his eyes and letting himself fall back into gentle sleep.

# Chapter 36

Longarm overslept. He missed the first two train connections and had to hustle in order to get his prisoners to the depot in time for the third southbound train of the day. The truth was that he did not mind at all.

"How much do I owe you for their keep?" he asked Charlie Logan when he got to the jail around mid-morning.

"Don't worry about it. We'll bill the Justice Department, same as always."

"That's okay for the big guy, but I'm paying cash for Bowman's meals. He's being transferred sort of unofficial-like. Favor for Billy Vail."

"Hell, Longarm, if it's a favor for Billy, don't you worry about it. We can cover two lousy meals for him."

"I can pay."

"Yes, and so can I. I like Billy, too, you know."

"I'm not gonna argue the point with you, Charlie, but I'll sure tell Billy about your kindness when I get t' the office."

"When you do, tell the old bastard hello from me and the sheriff. We'd both like to see him the next time he's in town."

"I'll do that. Did my boys give you any trouble last night?" Longarm put his wallet back into his coat pocket.

Charlie grinned. "The big one kept yammering about being hungry. I just shut the door so his noise wouldn't bother me. He quieted down some after a while."

"Nobody came around looking to see him?"

"Not him. We did turn away some visitors for Roberto Gutierrez and Jesus Martinez, but I knew both of the fellas as were wanting to visit. There's no harm in those two. And the jailer tells me after I went home last night there was somebody here asking for Edward Bowman. Didn't you tell me the man's name is Edgar? That's what I wrote down on my daily report anyhow."

"His name is Edgar."

"Then whoever wanted to see him must not know him too good," Charlie said.

"Prohb'ly heard the name Ed and assumed the full of it was Edward. And just as prob'ly it was Jones he wanted to see. Wanted to put a bullet into him more 'n likely."

"The jailer said this fella was getting pretty insistent, but about then, the city night marshal dropped in for a cup of coffee and the visitor left. He didn't come back."

"Could have been another assassination attempt," Longarm said.

Charlie shrugged. "No way to tell now."

"Did the jailer say who the man was or what he looked like?"

"Said he was a gentleman sort. Wore a suit and a nice hat that was never used to rub a horse down or to carry water. I did ask but he didn't remember anything more."

"All right, Charlie, thanks. I'll keep my eyes open. The good thing is that we won't be so awful long getting to

Denver. If you'll trot 'em out now, I'll put the 'cuffs on them and sign for the prisoners."

"I'll have them out here in two shakes of a lamb's tail." Charlie grinned and added, "Or three shakes of a limp dick, which is a lot more fun than some dang lamb tails."

Longarm chuckled and reached into his hip pocket for a pair of handcuffs.

The trip back home to Denver was uneventful despite Longarm's worries about a last-minute attempt on Tomlin Jones's life. No one—male, female or otherwise—seemed the least bit interested in their little group. They arrived safely just at dusk.

"I'm hungry," Jones complained as he and Bowman came gingerly down the portable steps, the two of them hampered by the handcuffs that connected them.

"You'll eat when I get you in the jail. Won't nobody be able to reach you in there."

Jones grumbled a little more, but the idea of being safe behind stone walls for the moment overcame his appetite.

"Excuse me, but what about me?" Bowman asked. "Will I be in jail again tonight, too?"

"No, we'll get Jones settled, then find a hack and drive out to Billy's house." He smiled. "I know your cousin is mighty anxious t' see you."

"No more than I am to see her again, I assure you."

Longarm hailed the first cab he saw when they walked out of the train depot but another man dashed out of the station and climbed into it first. "Grant and Colfax. I'm in a hurry," Longarm heard him say. The intersection was in the heart of Denver's government buildings. Probably the rude SOB was a legislator or some such, politicians being among the pushiest and most arrogant folk Longarm knew and never mind their supposed service to their constituents and their country. The way he saw it they were nearly all of them hogs feeding at the public trough.

Before he could look around for another hackney, one pulled to the curb, the driver apparently having seen the other coach grabbed first.

"Where away, gents?"

Longarm ushered Bowman and Jones inside the closed carriage, then stepped up himself. "Denver county jail," he told the driver, "and I'll want you to wait an' carry two of us on after that. I'll pay for your time waiting."

"Very well, sir. Whatever you require."

Longarm pulled the door closed behind him, and the cab started forward with a lurch.

# Chapter 37

Longarm felt a deep relief once he got Tomlin Jones settled securely inside the Denver county jail. No assassin was going to get to the man there. It was a considerable weight off his mind.

"Look a' here, Ed. You've been no trouble this whole time. If you're willing to give me your word you won't try to run, I don't see any need to be putting 'cuffs on you again." He smiled. "Biggest reason I been doing it so far is so's you would anchor Jones in place. Now that man, he can run. I wouldn't doubt he could stay ahead of a horse in a race that lasted a while. They say a man can do that anyhow, and if any human being can then I think it'd likely be Tomlin Jones."

"You'd trust a lunatic?" Bowman asked.

"It strikes me that you haven't exactly been barking at the moon or nothing like that, Ed. Mayhap you aren't quite as crazy as I was led t' believe."

"Why . . . thank you. You and Bob Jessup are the only two people I've known in an awfully long time who didn't

171

act like they expected me to foam at the mouth and try to bite someone. And if you want my parole, I will be proud to give it to you." He grinned. "Besides, I don't have any money on me nor any idea where the Vails live. Since your intention is to take me exactly where I want to go, it is in my best interest to stay with you, isn't it?"

"Ha! Reckon I'll reserve judgment on how crazy you are, Ed, but I can say without contradiction that you're no fool. An' you're exactly right about us both wanting you back with the Vails. Let's find that hack that's waiting for us and go over to the federal building. Billy works late more often than not. We might just catch him there, and the office isn't as far as their house. Right on the way to the house, too."

Bowman thanked the jailers who had taken charge of Jones and led the way outside. The hack driver was right where they left him a half hour before, dozing on the driving box while his horses stood hip-shot and sleepy.

"Thanks for waiting," Longarm said as Ed climbed inside the hack.

"My pleasure. Where to now, mister?"

"Federal building."

The driver picked up his reins and waggled them to shift the bits in the horses' mouths and tell them to wake up and tend to business. Longarm stepped into the coach and pulled the door shut and they were off.

A few minutes later, the hack wheeled in a U-turn and came to a halt in front of the familiar stone steps. "Federal building, Marshal," the driver called out.

"All right, thanks." Longarm got out, Ed Bowman helpfully following with Longarm's carpetbag in hand. "How much do I owe you?"

"I'd say, oh, four dollars ought to cover it."

"Fine." Longarm sorted through the change in his pocket until he found a five-dollar half eagle and handed it up to the man. "Keep the change."

"Thanks, mister."

Longarm bent down and whispered in Ed Bowman's ear, "Move straight to the steps. Stay exactly in front of me. Don't wander to either side, y' hear? And when I shout, you get up them steps just as fast as you can. Get inside and outta sight. I'll be right behind."

"But what . . . ?"

"Never mind the palaver. Just do what I say. Do it now."

Longarm gave Bowman a little push in the back and quickly followed when the slender engineer walked forward.

Behind him he heard the springs of the hackney creak as the weight shifted on the rig.

Longarm was already turning, Colt in hand, by the time the cab driver brought the shotgun out from under his lap robe and tried to point the ugly weapon down at Longarm and Edgar Bowman.

# Chapter 38

The thunder of Longarm's .44-40 reverberated off the granite walls of the federal building and the nearby U.S. Mint. Flame and smoke filled the air.

The hack driver cried out, a bullet lodged deep in his chest, while the left barrel of the shotgun discharged, adding to the smoke and the fire.

Longarm heard lead balls splatter onto the paving stones like hail. He felt one tug at the cuff of his trouser leg. He aimed the Colt through the swirling smoke and fired again, this time taking his time and making it a killing shot into the man's forehead. There was, after all, a loaded barrel remaining in that scattergun.

The shotgun clattered harmlessly onto the floor of the cab's driving box while the shooter fell back lifeless onto the seat. The startled horses bolted but Ed Bowman grabbed the cheek strap of the off horse and dragged it to a halt almost before they had time to begin.

The horses were walleyed and nervous but Bowman

calmed them, then dragged the reins down and tied them around a lamppost.

"That was quick thinking," Longarm said, "but what the hell were you doing jumping at the coach like that? Shouldn't you have been running the hell the other way?"

Bowman shrugged and grinned. "It seemed like a good idea at the time."

"Yeah, well next time, if there is a next time, leave the shooting t' me. You get the hell outta the way and . . . get down!"

Longarm grabbed Bowman by the arm and dragged him back behind the horses. Across the street a man was leaning out of the side window of another hackney. He had a gun in his hand and it was pointing toward the lamppost where Ed Bowman had been standing.

The man in the cab was handsomely dressed in coat and tie and wore a hat with a narrow brim. He looked like a businessman. Longarm was fairly sure he had seen the fellow before but he could not recall where.

The gent withdrew inside the coach and leaned to the side to call up to the cab driver.

Longarm dashed out into the street toward the front of that hack to get the driver's attention. "Don't you be going anywhere." The cabbie reined in his team and set the brake.

Shifting his attention to the passenger, Longarm said, "You and me are gonna talk, mister. Come outta there, an' I'll thank you t' do it with your hands empty."

"Yes, of course. I will come out. Don't shoot. Just don't shoot, Marshal."

Now dammit, Longarm thought, that was two men in the space of two minutes who knew he was a deputy marshal when neither one of them had cause to. First, the now-dead hack driver called him that—which should have been

176

a warning, but he didn't pay it any particular mind at the time—and now this fellow, too.

And the man in this cab was there waiting and watching when the driver of the other rig tried to shoot . . . tried to shoot just exactly *who*?

Tomlin Jones was comfortably locked away over at the county jail, so this ambush had nothing to do with him. And Longarm was not involved in any cases at the moment that would have gentlemen in suit coats gunning for him.

That left Edgar Bowman. Could he have been the target of those other shootings? Except that would not account for the gunman back in Fannin who made a try in that saloon.

This didn't make sense.

Still, this time Longarm had a live one who he could have a few words with.

He moved around to the front of the cab and stepped up onto the sidewalk so he would be on the same side of the coach as the door.

"Step down outta that cab, mister. And don't be showin' no gun or I will be obliged to ruin that nice suit o' yours with blood an' bullet holes."

"I'm coming out now. Don't shoot. Don't shoot."

# Chapter 39

The gent came down from the coach very carefully, hands raised, one of them holding his revolver by the barrel and upside down at that. "Don't shoot me now."

"I ain't gonna shoot. Just get down an' lay that weapon aside."

"Whatever you say, Marshal. Oh!" He tripped and grabbed for the door frame to keep himself from falling.

Except he was in perfect balance and feigned the fall as an excuse to whip his hands—and that revolver—downward.

"Don't," Longarm ordered.

The stupid son of a bitch wasn't half quick enough with his silly trick.

Longarm shot him. Once in the belly and again high in the chest. The fellow's gun fell onto the sidewalk and discharged, the bullet skittering along the ground and striking the off horse in a rear hoof. The horse squealed and tried to dance away from the pain.

The driver came down from his box in a hurry, cussing and trying to comfort his ruined animal.

Longarm thought for an instant that this cab driver, too, intended taking a hand in whatever game was being played here and came damn-all close to shooting him, but the fellow only wanted to reach his injured horse.

The gent with the evil intentions dropped to his knees and then toppled face forward onto the sidewalk.

Longarm warily approached. He kicked the fallen pistol aside, then stood over the man and held the muzzle of his Colt to the nape of the fellow's neck while he reached around to his throat and felt for a pulse.

He found only a faint flutter of movement there and after a few seconds that faded away. The gentleman was dead.

Longarm came upright and looked around for more danger and, seeing none, snapped open the loading gate of his Colt and quickly reloaded.

Henry, Billy Vail and Ed Bowman came around the back of the cab to join him.

"Uh huh," Longarm said to his boss. "Now that it's safe you show up."

"Custis, are you so worried about the population of Denver getting too big that you intend to start littering the streets with bodies?"

"Damn right. I intend t' cut down every single one o' them that shoots at me. Whether I know why they done it or not. An' in this case, Billy, I got no idea why either o' these fellas would be trying to shoot me."

"I can tell you about that one across the street," Vail said. "He was paid for the job. Had one hundred fifty dollars in shiny new coins in his pocket. And from the way this one is dressed, my guess is that he is the one who did the hiring. Edgar tells me this is not the first incident you two have had."

"Yeah, but why would they keep on once Jones was in the jail? That's what I can't figure out."

"I'm afraid it is my fault," Bowman said.

"How's that?"

The engineer bent down and rolled the dead gent onto his back and peered into his face for a moment. "I thought so."

"What?"

"I know him. I'm afraid I was the target of all this."

"You, not Jones?"

"Yes. This man is a lawyer. I don't know exactly what position he holds with the company, but I know he is tied in with the management of the railroad I was working for before I was locked away."

"He's with the Union Pacific?"

"No, no. The Deseret and Great North Western. We were building a railroad from Ogden north into Idaho with plans eventually to go on to Puget Sound."

"All right, but what does that have to do with anything?" Longarm asked.

"I didn't tell you about it, Deputy, because I assumed you would not listen to anything a madman had to say. You told me you were taking me back to Billy and Pip. I knew they would listen to what I had to say, so I kept my mouth shut. I suppose now that I should have told you, but at the time . . ." He spread his palms and shrugged.

"Shoulda told us what?"

"My employers locked me in that asylum because I learned something I should not have. When that plan failed I guess they decided it was better to have me killed than to let me tell what I knew."

"Which is?"

"The planned route passes through several lovely valleys, you see. The problem is that the railroad does not own

181

the right-of-way in those valleys where I was laying out the route and designing the bridges. Their right-of-way lies in extremely rugged country where the costs of construction would be ten, perhaps twelve times as high. So they shifted the line west far enough to lower their costs and increase their profits. To do that they intended building on land that is part of an Indian reservation. They did not bother to seek permission from the tribe nor from the government. I suppose they thought that would be too expensive, too. It would be cheaper and easier to build the road where they wanted it. After all, it was empty land not really being used by the Indians. They probably thought no one would ever notice. Then I did. And they locked me away in . . . that place." He shuddered.

"God, Pug, why didn't you tell us?" Billy said.

"My mail was censored, Bill. I had no way to tell you. So"—he smiled—"I escaped."

"Why in the world did you go west when you were free? Why didn't you come to us at once?"

"I would have, but I assumed they would expect me to come to Denver. I intended to go to California, you see, and write you from there. I just got sidetracked a little along the way."

"But dammit," Longarm said, "that fellow who shot at me back in Fannin couldn't know I was comin' t' get you."

"Sheriff Stone sent a wire about him, Longarm. Do you know of a fugitive named Abner Helm?"

"Never heard of him."

"Well, he seems to have heard of you. He was wanted in California on charges of murder and rape. He had nothing to do with this. Probably thought you were there because of him."

"If he'd just turned and walked out the door that day, I

never would've noticed the dumb son of a bitch," Longarm said. "But what about Jones? Wasn't none of them after Jones?"

"Only for embezzlement, and that charge is back in Grady," Billy said. "Jones is no longer needed here. Delbert Staley accepted a plea bargain agreement with the U.S. attorney. Staley will plead guilty to lesser charges and will spend no more than six months in jail . . . no prison time at all, just the local jail where he will have friends . . . and make restitution to the government."

"So Jones . . ."

Billy smiled. "Can turn right around and go back to Nevada."

"Billy, surely you ain't thinking . . ."

"Get yourself a good night's rest, Custis. You can pick up your prisoner and start back tomorrow morning."

"Dammit, Billy!"

But Vail was ignoring him. The marshal draped an arm over Ed Bowman's shoulders and led him back toward the federal building. "Let me get my coat, and we'll go home, Edgar. I know someone who is very anxious to see you."

Henry nudged Longarm in the ribs. "Don't forget to come inside once you get these bodies carried away. You have some reports to complete, and I will want to get to work on your expense voucher so I can turn it in tomorrow, and then I'll need you to . . ."

But Longarm was no longer listening. He just stood there feeling sorry for himself.

Watch for

**LONGARM AND THE SIDEKICK
FROM HELL**

the 319<sup>th</sup> novel in the exciting LONGARM series

from Jove

*Coming in June!*

**Explore the exciting Old West with one of the men who made it wild!**

IN THIS GIANT-SIZED ADVENTURE,
AN OUTLAW LEARNS THAT HE'S
SAFER IN HIS GRAVE THAN
FACING AN AVENGING ANGEL
NAMED LONGARM.

0-515-13547-X

# JAKE LOGAN
## TODAY'S HOTTEST ACTION WESTERN!

# J. R. ROBERTS

# THE GUNSMITH